The X-Files
From HarperEntertainment

THE X-FILES: GOBLINS
THE X-FILES: WHIRLWIND
THE X-FILES: GROUND ZERO
THE X-FILES: ANTIBODIES
THE X-FILES: RUINS
THE X-FILES: SKIN

Coming Soon
From HarperEntertainment

THE X-FILES: I WANT TO BELIEVE

THE (X)-FILES™

WHIRLWIND

CHARLES GRANT

Based on the characters created by
Chris Carter

HARPER

ENTERTAINMENT
An Imprint of HarperCollinsPublishers

ENTERTAINMENT
An Imprint of HarperCollins*Publishers*
10 East 53rd Street
New York, New York 10022-5299

Copyright © 1995, 2008 by Twentieth Century Fox Film Corporation
Cover photograph copyright © 1994 by Twentieth Century Fox Corporation
Cover illustration by Rick Lieber
ISBN 978-0-06-105415-0

First HarperEntertainment paperback printing: July 2008
First HarperPrism paperback printing: June 1995

HarperCollins® and HarperEntertainment™ are trademarks of HarperCollins Publishers.

The X-Files™ is a trademark of Twentieth Century Fox Corporation.

Printed in the United States of America

Visit HarperEntertainment on the World Wide Web
at www.harpercollins.com

20 19

This is for Kathryn Ptacek.

For lots of reasons, but in particular, this time,
because I've mangled her New Mexico homeland
before, and she still hasn't shot me.

ACKNOWLEDGMENTS

My gratitude and fond appreciation to the poor folks who had to listen, advise, and humor me over the past few months:

Caitlin Blasdell, who, for reasons known only to herself, puts up with all my calls, and has never once told me to stop bugging her and get back to work;

Steve Nesheim, M.D., for the wonderfully gruesome details, and for all the possibilities therein;

Wendy Webb, R.N., M.Ed., for taking those details and actually making them fun;

Geoffrey Marsh, for graciously allowing me to borrow the Konochine Indians for my own disgusting use;

The Jersey Conspiracy, as always, this time providing me with more dead bodies than I could possibly use this time around, and one drunk;

And Robert E. Vardeman, who never stops reminding me why it's nice to have good friends in far places.

ONE

The sun was white and hot, and the wind blew ceaselessly.

Annie Hatch stood alone on her ranch house porch, one hand absently rubbing her stomach as she tried to decide what to do. The late-morning sun made her squint, the temperature already riding near ninety.

But the wind that coasted across the high desert made her wish, for the first time in a long time, that she were back in California.

It hissed softly through the brush, and whispered softly in her ear.

Of course, she thought; you could also just be a doddering old fool.

A quick smile, a quicker sigh, and she inhaled

slowly, deeply, taking in the heat, and the piñon, and, so faintly she might have been imagining it, a sweet touch of juniper.

Wind or not, voices or not, this was, all in all, far better than Hollywood.

That was where she and Burt had made their money, so many years ago it might have been a dream; here was where they had finally made their lives, no dream at all.

A breath of melancholy fluttered her eyelids closed for a moment. It wasn't easy being a widow, even after fifteen years. There were still too many times when she thought she heard him clumping back from the stable behind the house, or whistling as he fiddled with the generator, or blowing gently on the back of her neck.

The wind did that to her, too.

"Enough," she muttered, and strode impatiently to the end of the porch, leaned over the waist-high, rough-hewn rail, and looked down the side of the adobe house to the stable. She whistled twice, high, sharp, and loud, and giggled silently when she heard Nando curse, not very subtly letting her know he hadn't finished saddling Diamond yet, was she trying to get him trampled?

A second later he appeared in the open doorway, hands on his wide hips, glaring at her from under his time-beaten Stetson.

She waved gaily; he gestured sharply in disgust and vanished again.

"That's cruel," a soft voice said behind her.

She laughed as she turned. "He loves it, Sil, and you know it."

Silvia Quintodo looked at her skeptically for as long as she could. Then she grinned broadly, shaking her head as if at a child too angelic to be punished. She was a round woman, face and figure, with straight black hair forever caught in a single braid that hung down her back. Her skin was almost copper, her large eyes the color of a starlit night. Today, as always, she wore a loose, plain white dress that reached to mid-shin, and russet deerskin boots.

"You're staring," she scolded lightly.

Annie blinked. "I am? I'm sorry. My mind was wandering." She stared at the weathered floorboards. "I guess I'm just feeling my age today, dear."

Silvia rolled her eyes—*oh, please, not again*—and returned inside to prepare an early lunch.

Annie thanked her silently for not feeding the self-pity.

In truth, she knew she wasn't so bad for an old lady of sixty-one. Her face was narrow, accentuating green eyes and dark, not quite thick, lips; the lines there were more from the sun than her age. Her hair was white, but softly so, cropped short and brushed straight back over her ears. Practical, but still lovely. And her slender figure was such that, even after all these years, she was still able to turn more than a few heads whenever she drove into the city or up to Santa Fe.

It was good for her ego.

Oh brother, she thought; it's worse than I thought.

What it was, was one of those days that crept up on her now and then—when she missed Burt so much it burned. There was never any particular reason for it, no specific thing that jogged her memory. It just happened. Like today. And the only cure was to take Diamond and a canteen and ride into the desert.

Maybe, if she were brave enough, all the way to the Mesa.

Sure, she thought; and tomorrow I'll wake up and find Burt beside me in bed.

A snort behind her made her jump.

She whirled just as Diamond thrust his head over the rail, his nose catching her stomach and shoving her back a step.

"Hey!" she said with a scolding laugh. "Knock it off, you big jerk."

He was already in bridle and saddle, a short black horse with a rough diamond blaze between his eyes. Nando stood beside him, grinning, one hand on the animal's rump, his stained brown hat pushed back on his head.

"Serves you right," he told her smugly. He could have been Silvia's twin, not her husband, save for the ragged streaks of gray in his hair, and the fact that his broad blunt nose had been broken too many times for him to be rightly called handsome. Those who didn't know him figured him for an ex-boxer or an ex-Marine, not the foreman of a ranch that wasn't much of a ranch anymore.

Annie made a show of ignoring him and his rebuke. She adjusted her straw Western hat, fixed the strap under her chin, and swung her legs easily over the rail. Without pause or hesitation, she grabbed the horn and swung lightly into the saddle. Only then did she look down at him. "Not bad for an old lady, huh?"

"The day you get old, *Señora*," he answered solemnly, "is the day I stop shoveling horse shit for a living and start selling bad turquoise to the tourists up Santa Fe."

Diamond shook his mane impatiently.

A warm gust made them turn their heads, but not before she saw the expression on his face.

When he looked back, he was somber. "It talks."

"I wouldn't know."

He shook his head slowly, not quite sadly. "You know. You always know."

She grabbed the reins angrily. "I know nothing of the sort, Nando." She was prepared to cluck Diamond away when Nando tapped her leg. "Now what?"

He reached behind him and pulled out a canteen. Grinning again: "No rain, no water." He tucked it into the silver-studded saddlebag.

She thanked him with a brusque nod and guided Diamond across the side lawn to a break in the double split-rail fence she had painted white the year before. Once through, she followed it around to the front, checking the grass inside to see where it was dying.

Everywhere, she realized; everywhere.

Despite the extraordinarily expensive, undoubtedly wasteful belowground system her late husband had installed himself and had connected to one of the score of deep wells on the ranch, the grass seldom survived intact all the way through the summer. Still, she thought as the ranch drifted away behind her, wasteful or not, it was better than nothing.

At least it had color.

At least it had life.

"All right," she snapped to the shadow that rode beside her. "All right, that's enough, Annie, that's enough."

Her right hand held the reins lightly; her left hand rested on her thigh, and it trembled.

She ignored it, concentrating instead on the rolling land ahead, automatically checking for wind or flash-flood damage to the narrow wood bridges Burt and Nando had built across the several arroyos meandering across the four thousand acres, glancing to her right every so often at the high heat-brown hill that blocked the sun each morning. Like the exposed knobby root of an ancient, distant tree, it flanked the recently paved road that led east to the interstate and west to the Mesa.

To the reservation.

She couldn't see it from here.

The hill crossed the road a half-mile ahead, still high, still marked with thorned shrubs and tufts of grass sharp enough to slice through a palm, still studded with large brown rocks and partially buried boulders.

Like a wall to keep the rest of the world out.

Or to keep the Konochine in.

For some, however, it wasn't high enough or strong enough.

They left to see what the world outside looked like, to discover what the world had to offer besides life on a reservation.

For her, it was Burt, and a brief but lucrative career in Hollywood; for others, unfortunately, it was prejudice and pain, and ultimately, a grave too far from home.

Diamond shied suddenly, forcing her to pay attention, to glance quickly at the ground for signs of rattlesnakes. They'd be out now—the sun was high and warm enough—coiled deceptively still on whatever rocks they could find.

She saw none, and frowned her puzzlement when the horse began to prance, telling her he wasn't thrilled about approaching the ranch side of the hill.

That's when she saw the buzzards.

Five of them circled low near the two-lane road, and she mouthed a sharp curse as she nudged the horse in that direction. There weren't many cattle left; she had sold most of them off not long after Burt had died, and seldom replaced the ones she lost. Every so often, though, one of those remaining found a way through the barbed wire that marked their pastures. Sometimes they tumbled into an arroyo; sometimes a rattler got them; sometimes they just couldn't find the water or the food and simply gave up, laid down, and died.

Closer, and she saw a van parked on the sandy shoulder, on the far side of the fence that ran along the blacktop. Vague waves of ghostly heat shimmered up from the road, blurring the vehicle's outline.

"What do you think?" she asked Diamond. "Tourists?"

The desert beyond the Sandia Mountains was beautiful in a stark and desolate way, with flashes of color all the more beautiful because they were so rare. It was also a trap. It wasn't unusual for an unthinking tourist to pull over because he wanted to walk a little, stretch his legs, check things out. It also wasn't unusual for the heat, and deceptive distance, to combine to lose him.

One minute, you could see everything; the next, you were alone.

Sometimes he didn't make it back.

Another twenty yards, and Diamond pulled up short.

"Hey," she said. "Come on, don't be stupid."

He shook his head violently, reaching around to nip at her boot, a sign he wasn't moving another inch.

She glared helplessly at the top of his head, watching his ears twitch in agitation. Forcing him would serve no purpose. He was as stubborn as she, and most definitely stronger.

"Can you say 'glue'?" she muttered sourly as she swung out of the saddle and ordered him to stay put. "Idiot."

Dusting her hands on her jeans, she trudged toward the van, scanning the area for whoever it was who had been stupid enough to leave it.

She hadn't gone a dozen yards when she heard the flies.

Her stomach tightened in anticipation, but she didn't stop. A check of the fence revealed no breaks in the wire, no toppled posts. The van itself was a dusty dark green, streaked with long-dried mud.

"Hello?" she called, just in case.

The flies sounded like bees.

The wind nudged her from behind.

She stepped around a sprawling juniper, and

her left hand instantly clamped tightly to her stomach.

"Oh God," she whispered. "Dear Jesus."

It wasn't a lost cow.

There were two of them, and they lay face-down, arms and legs spread, unnaturally twisted. Flies crawled in undulating waves over them, thick and black, drifting into the air and drifting down again. Not five feet away, a buzzard watched, its wings flexing slowly.

It snapped its beak once.

Annie spun away and bent over, hands on her knees, eyes shut and stomach lurching, her throat working hard to keep the bile from rising.

She knew the bodies were human.

But only by their shape.

Even with the flies, even with the sun, it was clear they had been skinned.

TWO

The sun was white and hot, and there was no wind.

Traffic in the nation's capital moved sullenly and loudly, while pedestrians, if they moved at all, glowered absently at the ground, praying that the next building they entered had its air conditioning working. In this prolonged July heat wave, that wasn't always the case.

Tempers were short to nonexistent, crimes of passion were up, and blame for the extreme discomfort was seldom aimed at the weather.

The office in the basement of the J. Edgar Hoover Building was, according to some, a working monument to the struggle of order over chaos.

It was long, not quite narrow, and divided in half by the remains of a floor-to-ceiling glass partition from which the door had long since been removed. Posters and notices were tacked and taped to the walls, and virtually every flat surface was covered by books, folders, or low stacks of paper. The lighting was dim, but it wasn't gloomy, and as usual, the air conditioning wasn't quite working.

In the back room, two men and a woman stared at a series of red-tabbed folders lying on a waist-high shelf. Each was open to the stark black-and-white photograph of a naked corpse, each corpse lying in the center of what appeared to be a tiled bathroom floor.

"I'm telling you, it's driving us nuts," the first man complained mildly. He was tall, solid, and a close-cropped redhead. His brown suit fit too snugly for real comfort. His tie had been pulled away from his collar and the collar button undone, the only concessions he made to the barely moving air. He wiped a hand over a tanned cheek, wiped the palm on his leg. "I mean, I know it's a signature, but I'll be damned if I can read it."

"Oh, put your glasses on, Stan," the woman muttered. She was near his height, her rounded face smooth, almost bland, with thin lips, and narrow eyes under dark brows. Unlike his clothes, her cream linen suit could have been tailored. "That's no signature, it's just slashes, for crying out loud. You're the one who's driving us nuts."

Stan Bournell closed his eyes briefly, as if in prayer. He said nothing.

"It's the bathroom that's important," she continued, her voice bored. It was clear to the second man that she had been on this route a hundred times. She pulled a tissue from a pocket and dabbed at her upper lip. "It's easier to clean, it's too small for the victim to hide in or run around in, and—"

"Beth, Beth," Bournell said wearily, "I know that, okay? I've got eyes. I can see."

The second man stood between them, hands easy on his hips. His jacket was draped over a chair in the other room with his tie, and the sleeves of his white shirt were rolled back twice. His face was unlined, and his age could have been anywhere from his late twenties to his mid-thirties, depending on how generous the estimate was.

Right now, he felt more like fifty.

The bickering had begun the moment the two agents had stormed into the office; the sniping had begun once the folders had been laid out.

He took a step away from them, closer to the work shelf.

They were both right.

He had read the files several days ago, at his
Section Head's request, but he didn't tell the
agents that; their tempers were frayed enough
already.

He sniffed, and rubbed a thoughtful finger
alongside his nose.

All five victims—or at least, the five the FBI
was thus far aware of—had first been attacked in
other rooms of their respective homes. Houses,
not apartments; suburbs, not cities. All signs indicated little or no struggle after the initial assault,
indicating knowledge of the attacker, or near-total
surprise. They had been chloroformed just
enough for immobility, then dragged elsewhere.
All were women, all in their early twenties, and
all had been murdered in their bathrooms.

Strangled with either an unfinished belt or
rawhide strap, their bodies stripped to the waist,
and a razor taken to their chests.

One slice each.

None had been raped.

Beth Neuhouse groaned and plucked at her
blouse. "God, doesn't the air conditioning work
in here? How can you work like this? It's like a
sauna."

Fox Mulder shrugged unconcern, then pushed
a hand back through his hair.

He checked each black-and-white in turn, his
gaze flicking over them increasingly rapidly, as
though he were reading.

"Well?" Bournell asked. "You got a magic trick for us? You got a rabbit we can chase?"

Mulder held up a hand to hush him, then slid the pictures from their folders and laid them out in a line. A moment later he switched the second and fourth.

"Mulder," Neuhouse said, "we haven't got all day. Either you've got something or you don't. Don't play games, okay?

Mulder straightened, and almost smiled. "Beth, get me a sheet of paper, please?" His left hand gestured vaguely toward the other room.

It was his tone that moved her more than the request. Those who had worked with him before had heard it at least once. One of the older agents had said it was like the first bay of a hound that had finally found the scent; you didn't argue with it, you just followed.

And you made sure your gun was loaded.

Bournell frowned. "What? I don't see it."

Mulder pushed the photographs closer together and pointed. "It's there. I think." Sudden doubt made him hesitate. "I'm—"

"Here." Neuhouse thrust a blank sheet into his hand. She stared at the bodies then, and her voice quieted. "I've been looking at those women for over a month, Mulder. I'm seeing them in my sleep."

He knew exactly what she meant.

In many ways, the black-and-whites were as bad as looking at the bodies themselves. Although the color was gone, violent death wasn't. The only thing missing was the smell, and it wouldn't take much effort to bring that up, too.

"So what do we have?" Bournell asked.

"I'm not positive. It's kind of crazy."

Neuhouse laughed quietly. "Well, this is the place for it, right?"

Mulder smiled. No offense had been meant, and he hadn't taken any. He knew his reputation in the Bureau, and it no longer bothered him. He was a flake, a maverick, a little around the bend on the other side of the river. He worked as much from logic and reason as anyone else, but there were times when he didn't have to take every single step along the way.

There were times when abrupt intuitive leaps put him ahead of the game.

Sometimes that was far enough to have it called magic.

Or, more often than not, spooky.

He put up with it because that reputation came in handy once in a while.

"Come on, Houdini," Bournell complained. "I'm frying in here."

Beth aimed a semiplayful slap at his arm. "Will you shut up and let the man think?"

"What think? All he has to do is—"

"Here," Mulder said, slapping the paper onto the shelf, indecision gone. He grabbed a pen from his shirt pocket. "Look at this."

The others leaned over his shoulders as he pointed to the first picture, but she wasn't the first victim. "The cut runs from just over her right breast to just under the left. In the next, it's the reverse."

"So?" Bournell said.

Mulder pointed again. "It could be the killer leans over and just cuts her." He straightened suddenly, and the others jumped back when his left hand demonstrated an angry, senseless slashing. "It could be, but I don't think so. Not this time." He pointed at the third woman. "This is clearly most of a letter, right?"

"R, maybe, if you combine it with the next one over," Neuhouse answered, glancing at her partner, daring him to contradict. "I know that much."

"Damn sloppy, then," Bournell said.

"For God's sake, Stan, he's slashing her! What the hell do you expect?"

Mulder copied the slash marks onto the paper, turned, and held it up.

They stared at it, puzzled, then stared at him—Bournell in confusion, Neuhouse with a disbelief that had her lips poised for a laugh.

"He's writing his name," Mulder told them. "He's letting you know who he is." He exhaled loudly. "One piece at a time."

*   *   *

The luncheonette was two blocks from FBI head-quarters, a narrow corner shop with a long Formica counter and a half-dozen window booths, most of the decor done in pale blues and white. The windows had been tinted to cut the sun's glare, but it still threatened Mulder with a drumming headache whenever he glanced out at the traffic.

Once done with the sparring duo, he had grabbed his tie and jacket and fled, stomach growling unmercifully, his head threatening to expand far beyond its limits. Even now he could hear them arguing, with each other and with him, telling him, and each other, that he was out of his freaking mind. Killers did not write their names on victims' bodies; at least, they sure didn't do it in classical Greek.

And when they finally, reluctantly, accepted it, they demanded to know who the killer was and why he did it.

Mulder didn't have any answers, and he told them that more than once.

When it had finally sunk in, they had stormed out as loudly as they'd stormed in, and he had stared at the door for nearly a full minute before deciding he'd better get out now, before the echoes of their bickering gave him a splitting headache.

The trouble was, stomach or not, the nattering and the heat had combined to kill his appetite.

The burger and fries looked greasy enough to be delicious, but he couldn't bring himself to pick anything up, even for a taste. Dumb, perhaps, but still, he couldn't do it.

A siren screamed; a police car raced down the center of the crowded street.

In the booth ahead of him, two couples chattered about baseball while at the same time they damned the heat wave that had been sitting on Washington for nearly two weeks.

On his right, on the last counter stool, an old man in a worn cardigan and golf cap listened to a portable radio, a talk show whose callers wanted to know what the local government was going to do about the looming water shortage and constant brownouts. A handful were old enough to still want to blame the Russians.

Mulder sighed and rubbed his eyes.

In calmer times, it was nice to know his expertise was appreciated; in times like these, exacerbated by the prolonged heat, he wished the world would leave him the hell alone.

He picked up a french fry and stared at it glumly.

The radio announced a film festival on one of the cable channels. Old films from the forties and fifties. Not at all guaranteed to be good, just fun.

He grunted, and popped the fry into his mouth. All right, he thought; I can hole up at home with Bogart for a while.

He smiled to himself.

The more he thought about it, the more he liked the idea. In fact, he thought as he picked up the burger, it sounded like exactly what he needed.

He was finished before he realized he had eaten a single bite. A good sign.

He grinned more broadly when a woman slipped into the booth and stared in disgust at his plate.

"You know," his partner said, "your arteries must be a scientific wonder."

He reached for the last fry, and Dana Scully slapped the back of his hand.

"Take a break and listen. We're wanted."

She was near his age and shorter, her face slightly rounded, light auburn hair settling softly on her shoulders. More than once, the object of one of their manhunts had thought her too feminine to be an obstacle. Not a single one of them had held that thought for very long.

Mulder wiped his mouth with a napkin, the grin easing to a tentative smile. "Wanted?"

"Skinner," she told him. "First thing in the morning. No excuses."

The smile held, but there was something new in his eyes. Anticipation, and a faint glimmer of excitement.

Assistant Director Skinner asking for them now, while they were both in the midst of cases still pending, generally meant only one thing.

Somewhere out there was an X-File, waiting.

"Maybe," she said, as if reading his mind. She snatched the last fry and bit it in half. An eyebrow lifted. "Or maybe you're just in trouble again."

THREE

X Twilight promised the desert, and the city at the base of the Sandia Mountains, a pleasantly cool evening. The heat had already begun to dissipate, and a wandering breeze raised wobbly dust devils along the interstate that stretched from Albuquerque to Santa Fe. Snakes sought their dens. A roadrunner streaked through a small corral, delighting a group of children who didn't want to leave their riding lessons. A hawk danced with the thermals.

On the low bank of the Rio Grande, beneath a stretch of heavy-crowned cottonwoods, Paulie Deven snapped pebbles and stones at the shallow water, cursing each time he hit the dried mud instead.

He hated New Mexico.

The Rio Grande was supposed to be this wide awesome river, deep, with rapids and cliffs, all that good stuff.

But not here. Here, he could almost spit across it, and most of the time it hardly held any water. You could forget about the cliffs, and rapids were out of the question.

He threw another stone.

Behind him, he could hear muffled music coming from the trailer his parents had rented from the developer until their new house was finished. That was supposed to have been three months ago, when they had arrived from Chicago. But some kind of permits were wrong, and then there was some kind of strike, and . . . and . . . He snarled and threw another rock, so hard he felt a twinge in his shoulder.

He thought he was going to live in the West. Maybe not the Old West, but it was supposed to be the West.

What his folks had done was simply trade one damn city for another. Except that he had belonged back in Chicago; back there the kids didn't get on his case because of the way he looked and sounded.

A light fall of pebbles startled him, but he didn't look around. It was probably his pain-in-the-ass sister, sliding down the slope to tell him Mom and Dad wanted him back in the trailer now, before some wild animal dragged him into the desert and ate him for breakfast.

Right.

Like there was anything out there big enough to eat something built like a football player.

"Paulie?"

He glanced over his left shoulder. "You blind, or what?"

Patty sneered and plopped down beside him. She was a year younger than his seventeen, her glasses thick, her brain thicker, her hair in two clumsy braids that thumped against her chest. He wasn't exactly stupid, but he sure felt that way whenever she was around.

She pulled her legs up and hugged her knees. "Not much of a river, is it?"

"Good eyes."

"They're fighting again."

Big surprise.

Ever since they had moved into the trailer, they had been fighting—about the house, about the move, about his Dad being close to losing his job, about practically anything they could. A damn war had practically started when he'd taken some of his savings and bought himself an Indian pendant on a beaded string. His father called him a goddamn faggot hippie, his mother defended him, and Paulie had finally slammed outside before his temper forced him to start swinging.

Patty rested her chin on her knees and stared at the sluggish water. Then she turned her head. "Paulie, are you going to run away?"

He couldn't believe it. "What?"

She shrugged, looked back at the river. "The way you've been acting, I thought . . . I don't know . . . I thought maybe you were going to try to get back to Chicago."

"I wish." He threw another rock; it hit the mud on the far side. "You ever think about it?"

"All the time."

That amazed him. Patty was the brain, the one with the level head, the one who never let anything get to her, ever. He hated to admit it, but he had lost count of the number of times she had saved his ass just by talking their folks into forgetting they were mad. Running away, running back home, was his kind of no-brain plan, not hers.

The sun died.

Night slipped from the cottonwoods.

A few stray lights from the trailer, from the handful of others on the other lots and the homes on the far side, were caught in fragments in the river, just enough to let him know it was still there.

Suddenly he didn't like the idea of being alone. "You're not going to do it, are you?"

She giggled. "You nuts? Leave this paradise?" She giggled again. "Sorry, Paulie, but I've got two years till graduation. I'm not going to screw it up, no matter what." She turned her head again; all he saw was her eyes. "But then, I swear to God, I'm going to blow this town so goddamn fast, you won't even remember what I look like."

He grinned. "That won't be hard."

"And the horse you rode in on, brother."

"I hate horses, too. Their manure smells like shit."

A second passed in silence before they exploded into laughter, covering their mouths, half-closing their eyes, rocking on their buttocks until Patty got the hiccups, and Paulie took great pleasure in thumping her back until she punched his arm away.

"I'm serious," she insisted, her face flushed. "I'm not kidding.

"Yeah, well." He watched the black water, rubbed a finger under his nose. "So am I."

Angry voices rose briefly above the music.

A door slammed somewhere else, and a pickup's engine gunned to launch the squealing of tires.

Off to their left, beyond the last tree, something began to hiss.

Paulie heard it first and frowned as he looked upriver, trying to see through the dark. "Pat?"

"Huh?"

"Do snakes come out at night?"

"What are you talking about? What snakes?"

He reached over and grabbed her arm to hush her up.

Hissing, slow and steady, almost too soft to hear.

"No," she whispered, a slight tremor in her voice. "At least, I don't think so. It's too cool, you know? They like it hot, or something."

Maybe she was right, but it sure sounded like snakes to him. A whole bunch of them, over there where none of the lights reached, about a hundred feet away.

Patty touched his hand, to get him to release her and to tell him she heard it, too. Whatever it was.

They couldn't see a thing.

Overhead, the breeze coasted through the leaves, and he looked up sharply, holding his breath until he realized what it was.

That was another thing he hated about this stupid place: it made too many sounds he couldn't identify, especially after sunset.

Every one of them gave him the creeps.

The hissing moved.

Except now it sounded like rapid, hoarse whispering, and Paulie shifted up to one knee, straining to make out something, anything, that would give him a clue as to who was out there and what they were doing.

Patty crawled up behind him, a hand resting on his back. "Let's get out of here, Paulie, huh?"

He shook his head obstinately. It was bad enough he was here because his folks had had some shit-for-brains idea about starting over, when they already had a perfectly good business back up North. He definitely wasn't going to let the buttheads here frighten him off.

City boy.

They called him "city boy" at school, their lips curled, their voices sneering, unimpressed by his size or the glares that he gave them.

Yeah, sure. Like this wasn't a city, right? Like they didn't have traffic jams, right? Like people didn't shoot and stab and stomp each other here like they did in Chicago, right?

The dark moved.

The hissing moved.

"Paulie?"

He swayed to his feet, trying not to make too much noise. His hands wiped across his jeans and curled into fists. Now they had made him angry.

"Paulie, come on."

"Go back up," he ordered without turning around.

Something had definitely moved out there, probably a bunch of wiseass kids trying to creep toward him. He took a sideways step up the uneven bank; his foot nudged a short length of dead branch. Without taking his eyes off the dark, he reached down and picked it up.

"Paulie."

"Go up!" he snapped, louder than he'd intended. "Damnit, Patty."

Staring so hard made him dizzy. It was like trying to pin down the edges of a black fog.

His free hand rubbed his eyes quickly and hard, but nothing changed.

There just wasn't enough light.

This, he thought, is really dumb. Get your ass outta here before something happens.

An arm snaked over his shoulder, and he bit so hard on a yelp that he choked.

Patty's hand opened to show him the dim gleam of a gold cigarette lighter. He took it and half-turned, his expression demanding to know when she'd started smoking. He realized the ridiculous timing when she flashed him a *not now, stupid* grin and jerked her chin to turn him back around.

His own smile had no humor.

He shifted the branch club until it felt properly balanced. Then he took a bold step forward and squared his shoulders. "Listen, assholes, you want to get lost, you want to get hurt, your choice."

No one answered.

Only the hissing.

He held the lighter up and sparked it, squinting

against the reach of the flame's faint yellow glow until his vision adjusted. There were shadows now that slid away and slid toward him as he raised the light over his head and moved his arm from side to side. The trees moved; the leaves turned gray; the bank took on contours that didn't exist.

"Hey!"

Another step.

"Hey!"

Another.

The breeze touched the back of his neck and twisted the flame to make the shadows writhe.

They kept coming, still whispering, and he gripped the club more tightly, angling it away from his leg, ready to swing at the first face that broke through the dark into the light. It wouldn't be the first time he smacked a homer with just one arm.

A low branch brushed leaves across his right cheek and shoulder before he could duck away.

He thought he heard Patty snap his name, but he wasn't sure. All sound had been reduced to his sneakers sliding over the ground, to the breeze tucked into the branches, and to the whispering.

He frowned.

No; it wasn't whispering.

It was, as he'd first thought, hissing. But strange. It wasn't like snakes at all, but like something . . . no, a lot of things brushing roughly over a rough surface.

Voices whispering.

He faltered, and licked his lips.

Okay, so maybe it wasn't people out there, and Patty said it probably wasn't snakes, and it sure wasn't the river.

So what the hell was it?

The breeze moved the leaves, and he looked up quickly, looked back and smiled.

That's what it was—someone dragging a branch along the ground. Leaves; the hissing was the leaves.

Growing louder.

Suddenly the lighter grew too hot to hold. He cursed soundlessly and let the flame die, whipping his hand back and forth to cool his fingers off, and the metal, so he could use it again in a hurry.

Timing now was everything.

He would wait until the asshole was close enough, then he'd turn on the light and swing at the same time. The jerk would never know what hit him.

He listened, a corner of his mouth twitching, his body adjusting slightly so that he was almost in a baseball stance.

Batter up, he thought; you goddamn freaks.

Louder.

No footsteps yet, but that didn't matter.

He checked back, but couldn't see his sister; he looked ahead, and made out a faint shadow that, because of virtually absent light, seemed taller than it ought to be.

Louder.

Very loud.

City boy, he thought angrily, and flicked on the lighter.

He didn't swing.

His sister screamed.

He couldn't swing.

His sister shrieked.

So did Paulie.

FOUR

Assistant Director Walter Skinner sat behind his desk, hands folded loosely in his lap, and stared absently at the ceiling for several seconds before lowering his gaze. He was not smiling. On the desk, in the center of the blotter, was an open folder. He looked at it disdainfully, shook his head once, and took off his wire-rimmed glasses. Thumb and forefinger massaged the bridge of his nose.

Mulder said nothing, and in the chair beside him, Scully's expression was perfectly noncommittal.

So far, the meeting hadn't gone well.

The entire transcript of a six-month wiretap on a Mafia don in Pittsburgh had been misplaced, and Mulder, arriving first, had walked straight into the teeth of the storm Skinner directed at his secretary and several red-faced agents. Mulder had been the target of the man's temper before, and he slipped hastily into the inner office with little more than a *here I am* nod.

Then he had committed the protocol error of taking a seat without being asked. When Skinner walked in, his face flushed with exasperation, Mulder wasn't quick enough to get to his feet, and the Assistant Director's curt greeting wouldn't have melted in a blast furnace.

It had been all downhill from there, even after Scully arrived, with Skinner raging quietly against those whose carelessness had imperiled an important investigation.

Mulder bore it all without comment.

At least the man wasn't raging against him for a change, which had not always been the case in the past.

Then, as now, the bone of contention between them was usually the X-Files.

The FBI's law enforcement mandate covered a multitude of federal crimes, from kidnapping to extortion, political assassination to bank robbery; it also permitted them to investigate local cases when local authorities asked them for assistance and the affair was such that it might be construed to be of potential federal interest, generally involving national security.

Not always, however.

Occasionally there were some cases that defied legal, sometimes rational, definition.

Cases that seemed to include instances of the paranormal, the inexplicable and bizarre, or the allegation that UFO activity was somehow involved.

X-Files.

They were Mulder's abiding, often single-minded, concern, and the core of his conviction that, X-File or not, the truth was not always as evident as it appeared to be. Nor was it always liberating or welcome.

But it was out there, and he was determined to find it.

And expose it.

The cost was immaterial; he had his reasons.

Skinner thumped a heavy hand on the folder. "Mulder . . ." He paused, the lighting reflecting off his glasses, banishing his eyes unnervingly until his head shifted. "Mulder, how in the name of heaven do you expect me to believe that this murderer is actually writing his name on his victims' chests?"

It was the tone more than the words that told him the Director was actually concerned about something else.

"I thought it was obvious, sir, once the patterns had been established."

Skinner stared at him for several seconds before he said, flatly, "Right."

A glance to Scully told Mulder he wasn't wrong about the Director's focus; it also told him he had somehow stepped on someone else's toes. Again. As usual.

He was, as he had told her more than once, a lousy Bureau dancer.

There in fact were few things that frustrated him more than internal Bureau politics. He supposed he should have known, given the personalities currently involved, that it would have been more politic to let either Neuhouse or Bournell come up with the solution on their own. He should have only been the guide. Suggesting instead of declaring.

And, given the personalities involved, he should have also guessed that one of them, probably Bournell, would have complained that Mulder was trying to steal the case, and thus the credit, from under them.

"Sir?" It was Scully.

Skinner shifted his eyes; the rest of him didn't move.

"As I understand it, there's a serious time constraint here. By his already established schedule, the killer is due to strike again within the next two weeks. Possibly sooner. Anything Agent Mulder is able to give them at this stage, any guidance he can offer, despite the pressure of his own caseload, can only be helpful, not an interference."

Mulder nodded carefully; his other reaction would have been to laugh.

"Besides," Scully added blandly as the Director replaced his glasses, "I doubt Mulder thinks this one is strange enough to tempt him."

Skinner looked at him, unblinking. "I can believe that, Agent Scully."

Mulder couldn't decipher the man's expression. He couldn't forget that it had been Skinner who had once shut down the X-Files on orders from higher up, from those who didn't like the way Mulder learned too much of what, from their point of view, didn't concern him; nor could he forget that it was Skinner who had ordered opened the X-Files again, and Mulder suspected the Director hadn't had much support.

It was confusing.

Skinner was neither all-out enemy nor all-out ally. Despite the profile of his position, he was a shadow, and Mulder was never quite sure what the shadow was, or what cast it.

"Excuse me, sir," he said carefully. "Am I being reprimanded for lending requested assistance?"

"No, Agent Mulder," the Director said wearily. "No, you're not." He rubbed the bridge again, this time without removing the glasses. "The record shows I called you in. It doesn't have to say what we talked about. But next time, do me a favor—save me some trouble and phone calls, and let someone else figure it out for a change. As Agent Scully suggested, be the guide."

He didn't smile.

Neither did the others.

Finally, he slapped the folder closed and indicated with a nod that they could leave. But as they reached the doorway, he added, "Greek, Mulder?"

"Classical Greek, sir."

The man nodded. "Of course."

Mulder resisted the temptation to salute and followed Scully into the hall, where she suggested coffee in the cafeteria, iced tea for him.

"You know," he said as they made their way down the hall, "I appreciate the support, Scully, but I don't need defending. Not really."

She looked up at him and sighed. "Oh yes you do, Mulder."

He looked back blankly.

"Trust me," she said, patting his arm. "On this one you'll have to trust me."

His temper didn't flare until later that afternoon.

He had been halfheartedly sorting through a half-dozen new cases dropped on his desk for evaluation. His Oxford-trained expertise in criminal behavior, and his natural talent for discovering patterns and traces where none seemed to exist, were natural magnets for investigations that had suddenly or inevitably run into a roadblock.

He didn't mind it; he enjoyed it.

What made him angry now was the admittedly unfounded suspicion that Bournell and Neuhouse had deliberately set him up for a reprimand. They were not incompetent. They were definitely not stupid. Given enough time, they would have undoubtedly seen what he had seen; and the Bureau was crawling with experts—either here in the city or out at Quantico—who could have reached the same conclusions.

He leaned back in his chair, stretched out his legs, and stared at the closed door.

A droplet of sweat rolled untouched down his cheek.

He couldn't help wondering if They were after him again—the unseen powers he had labeled the Shadow Government; the people who knew more than they let on about the truth he himself knew existed in the X-Files.

It wasn't paranoia.

On more than one occasion, they had tried to discredit him, and thus have him fired.

On more than one occasion, they had tried to kill him.

And Scully.

Only the fact that he had somehow attracted

friends in that same gray land of shifting shadows kept him alive and functioning, and he knew it.

Now it was possible They were at it again. Nibbling at him this time. Distracting him. Possibly hoping to force him into a careless mistake on one of the cases he needed to study. He had learned the hard way that there was only so much Skinner and the unknowns could do to protect him.

"I should have told them it was Russian," he whispered to the floor.

And laughed.

Suddenly the door slammed open, nearly spilling him out of the chair. Bournell stood on the threshold, pointing at him.

"Mulder, who knows old Greek?" the agent demanded hoarsely.

Mulder shrugged. "I don't know. Old Greeks?"

Bournell blinked slowly, took a step into the office just as a hush of cold air spilled out of the vents. He made as if to close the door behind them, and changed his mind. Instead, he slipped one hand into a pocket.

"Priests, Mulder. Seminarians. Teachers in a seminary. Preachers, Mulder. Ministers." His free hand took a slow swipe of his tie. "People, Mulder, who study the Bible."

Mulder waited patiently, unmoving. He suspected it wouldn't exactly do to mention that the list might also include professors of ancient languages, archaeology, and who knew what else. Not to mention immigrants who had been schooled in Greece. Or nonacademic scholars of at least a dozen different disciplines, both scientific and otherwise. The man was excited about something, and he didn't want to throw him off.

"I got to thinking," the agent continued, a finger tapping the face of the closest filing cabinet. "You were right about the Greek part, and I've kicked myself a dozen times for not noticing it before. But I have to tell you I think you're wrong about the name."

Mulder sat up slowly, drawing in his legs, tilting his head, eyes slightly narrowed. "How?"

"I was in a fraternity in college."

"A sorority would have been more fun."

Bournell glared at him in faint disgust until he lifted a hand in apology.

"Okay. So you were in a fraternity. What does that have to do with—"

"Alpha Chi Rho, it was." He held out his right hand; on it was an impressive signet ring, a faceted dark ruby centered in gold. He took a step closer so Mulder could see it more clearly. "On the rim, Mulder. Check out the rim."

He did, saw the three raised letters, and held his breath.

The hand dropped away. "Chi Rho. The symbol for Christ, Mulder." There was glee in his voice, in the way his hand danced at his side. "That's what he carved: Chi Rho." A sharp nod, a slap of the hand against his thigh. "Those women aren't hookers, that would be too easy. But I'll bet the farm and farmhouse there's something about them, a connection, that a religious fanatic might find to be . . . I don't know, sinful."

Mulder sat back, admiration clear. "I'll be damned."

Bournell smiled, rubbed his palms together, and glanced toward the vent. "Man, it's like an icebox in here. Your thermostat busted or what?" He headed for the door, grabbed the knob, and paused before leaving.

Mulder watched his shoulders tense, and relax.

"Hey, thanks, Mulder. No kidding. To be honest, I don't know if I really ever would have seen that Greek stuff. I've had this ring forever and hardly ever looked at it. But I just had it cleaned, and when I was putting it on this morning . . . well, it got me thinking, you know? And the next thing I knew I was looking at it like I'd never seen it before."

He hesitated, about to say something else, then nodded his thanks and closed the door behind him.

Mulder didn't move for a long time.

FIVE

X Sheriff Chuck Sparrow took off his hat, wiped a forearm over what was left of his hair, and slapped the hat back into place, yanking the brim down hard.

"What do you think?" the woman beside him asked, her voice tight with the effort not to lose her dinner.

Sparrow shook his head. The best he could figure, either somebody was in sore desperate need to practice his tanning skills, or there was another one of those damn cults holed up in the hills again. Either way, it didn't take a brain surgeon to see that he was in for a hell of a lot more work than his inclination wanted.

They stood side by side near the mouth of a small cave, on the west side of a solitary low hill two miles west of the Hatch ranch. Sprawled in front of it was what was left of a steer, ants and flies now vying for the right to rid the dead animal of whatever they could take.

"What do you think?"

"Donna," he said, "I wish to hell I knew."

She was a tall woman, her figure hidden in boots, baggy jeans, and a man's shirt about a size too large. Her short brown hair was brushed back over her ears, and on her right hand she wore the biggest silver ring Sparrow had ever seen. Her Cherokee was parked on the shoulder, fifty yards away; his patrol car was behind it.

She jutted her chin toward the cave. "You look in there?"

"Yes," he answered with exaggerated patience. "Yes, I looked in there."

"And?"

"And fourteen different kinds of shit is all what I found, all right? Bones. Little bones," he added hastily. "The usual crap."

"I read that they use them, you know. Kind of temporary, so to speak."

He scanned the hillside, squinted at the vehicles. "Now don't take this wrong, all right? But there hasn't been a damn mountain lion around here for nearly as long as I've been working this job. And in case you hadn't noticed, they don't generally skin their meals before they eat them."

"I don't need your sarcasm, Chuck."

No, he thought; what you need is a good swat upside the head, keep you from bothering the hell outta me.

The trouble was, this was the fourth animal he'd come across in just over a week slaughtered like this, and not a single sign, not a single print, not a single goddamn hint of what had killed them. Or rather, what had stripped off their hides. For no reason he could put a finger on, he didn't think they had been killed first. He reckoned the creatures had either died of the shock or had bled to death.

Just like he was about to die of the smell if he didn't get out of here.

He brushed a hand over his mouth as he turned and walked back to the car. Donna followed him slowly, humming to herself and snapping her fingers.

The thing of it was, Sparrow thought as he slid down the shallow ditch and took two grunting strides up the other side, if this was confined to just animals, there wouldn't be such a stink of another kind in the office.

That there were also three people dead, obviously of the same thing—whatever the hell that was—had put the fire on. So to speak. And every time someone called in with another claim, it was Sparrow who personally checked it out. It wasn't that he didn't trust any of his deputies. Thirty-five years roaming the side roads of the desert, talking to the Indians in Santo Domingo, San Felipe and the other pueblos, getting to know the hills and mountains until he could walk them practically blindfolded, did that to a man—made him the so-called area expert, even when he didn't want to be, hadn't asked to be, and would have given his right arm just to be plain stupid.

He reached in the driver's-side window and grabbed the mike, called in and told the dispatcher what he'd found and where. While Donna watched him distrustfully, he ordered a van to pick up the carcass, and a vet standing by to handle the examination. When he was finished, he dropped the mike onto the seat and leaned back against the door, arms folded across a chest nearly as broad as the stomach below it.

"You think you might go talk to Annie?" She stood in the middle of the two-lane road, sketching senseless patterns in the dust that turned the blacktop gray.

"What for?" He waved vaguely to his right. "Her place is too far away."

"Might be one of hers."

"Probably," he admitted. Then he gestured toward the hill, meaning what lay a mile or so beyond, what some of the locals called the Konochine Wall. "Might be one of theirs, too, you ever think of that?"

She didn't look, and he smiled. Donna Falkner didn't much care for the Konochine. For years they had refused her offers to broker whatever craftwork they wanted to sell; once they had even chased her off the reservation. Literally chased her, yelling and waving whatever came to hand, as if they wanted to drag her up Sangre Viento Mesa and drop her off, just as they had done to the Spanish priests and soldiers during the Pueblo Revolt over three hundred years before.

The difference was, the Spaniards never returned to the Konochine. No one knew why.

Now there was a middleman, Nick Lanaya, who worked with her, so she never had to set foot on the reservation at all.

"Satanists," Donna suggested then, still toeing the blacktop, hands in her hip pockets.

Sparrow snorted. He had been through the entire list of the usuals, from Satanists all the way to half-assed dopeheads who thought they could bring on a better world by chopping the heads off calves and goats. None of them, as far as he knew, killed like this, or killed both animals and people quite so ruthlessly and left the bodies behind.

But then, he wasn't an expert there, and he sighed as he finally admitted that maybe it was time to bring those experts in. Pride and getting nowhere fast were getting him crucified in the papers.

Two men sat on a hillside, their loose-fitting clothes as brown and tan as the ground around them. The first was old, his straight hair dull white and touching his bony shoulders. The planes of his face were sharp, the dark skin crevassed around the mouth and deep-set eyes. There was a necklace of rattlesnake spine around his neck.

The second man was much younger, but not young. His hair was still black, pulled back into a ponytail held by a braided circlet of gold and turquoise. His knees were drawn up, and his hands dangled between them, long fingers constantly moving like reeds in a slow wind.

When they spoke, which wasn't often, it was in a combination of bastard Spanish and Konochine.

"Father," the younger man said, attitude and voice deferential and weary, "you have to stop it."

The old man shook his head.

"But you know what he's doing. He's damning us all."

No answer.

The younger man reached for a tuft of grass, stopping himself just before he grabbed it. The blades were sharp; had he pulled, they would have drawn blood. He grabbed a stone instead and flung it hard down the slope.

Below was the road that led out of the gap, past

Annie Hatch's ranch to the interstate. Behind was Sangre Viento Mesa.

"People are dying, Dugan," he said at last, abandoning honorifics for first names. "He takes them as far away as Albuquerque now." He didn't turn his head; he knew the old man wasn't watching. "It's gotten too big to hide. They're going to come sooner or later, the authorities. We won't be able to keep them out."

The old man touched his necklace. "They can come, Nick. They can look. They won't find anything."

"And if they do?" the younger man persisted.

The old man almost smiled. "They won't believe it."

Donna watched the sheriff's car speed away, dust swirling into rooster tails from its rear tires. She knew his ego had taken a fierce beating because he hadn't yet been able to locate the cult behind the atrocities, but she didn't think he or the city police were looking in the right place. Haunting the downtown Albuquerque bars and sending undercover men to the university wasn't going to accomplish anything but pay out more overtime.

She squinted at the sky, saw nothing but a wisp of a cloud that looked lost amid all that washed-out blue.

The *Journal* and the *Tribune* were screaming for someone's blood, and if Sparrow didn't watch out, it was going to be his.

Not, she thought sourly as she headed back to her car, that it was any concern of hers. He was a big boy. He could take care of himself. Just because he never paid her any mind whenever she tried to give him a hand, just because he thought she was a little off-center, just because he never gave her the time of day unless she asked him right out . . .

"Shit," she said, and kicked at the Cherokee's front tire. "Idiot."

She swung herself in, hissing sharply when her fingers grabbed the hot steering wheel and snapped away. A pair of colorless work gloves lay on the passenger seat, and she slipped them on, glancing in the rearview mirror, then looking toward the hill and the cloud of flies that marked the steer's carcass. Her stomach lurched; a slow deep breath settled it.

This wasn't like her at all.

She had seen worse out in the desert, and much worse in town, after a knife fight or a shooting. She had no idea why this spooked her so much.

A quick turn of the key fired the engine, and another glance in the rearview nearly made her scream.

A pickup more rust and dust than red streaked directly toward her rear bumper, sunlight exploding from the windshield, the grill like a mouth of gleaming shark's teeth.

She braced herself for the impact, but the truck swerved at the last second, slowed abruptly, and passed her so sedately she wondered if it had really been speeding at all, if it hadn't been her imagination.

A look to her right, and the other driver stared back.

Oh God, she thought.

A gray hat pulled low, black sunglasses, long black hair in a ponytail that reached to the center of the man's back.

Leon Ciola.

She didn't realize she was holding her breath until the pickup disappeared ahead of the dust its tires raised; then she sagged against the seat, tilted her head back, and closed her eyes. Air conditioning spilled across her lap; she shivered but didn't turn it down or deflect it elsewhere. She kept her eyes closed until she couldn't stand it. When they opened, she was alone; even the dust had gone.

Go, she ordered as she swallowed dryly; go home, girl.

It took her ten minutes before she could take the wheel again without shaking, another ten minutes before she realized she wasn't moving and tromped on the accelerator, ignoring the machine gun that rattled beneath the carriage, fighting the fishtail until the vehicle straightened, and the sun made her blind to everything but the road.

Home first, and a drink. Then she would call Sparrow and tell him Ciola was back.

She had a feeling the sheriff would be royally pissed.

The younger man stood, mock-groaning as he rubbed the small of his back and stretched his legs to relieve the stiffness. He tried again:

"Dugan, we can't let this happen. It will ruin everything we've worked for."

The old man didn't rise, didn't look back. His gaze seemed to focus on the dust clouds in the distance. "We can't stop it, Nick."

"Maybe not, but we can stop him."

"We don't know for sure."

But damnit, we do, the younger man thought angrily; we know damn well it's him, and we're doing nothing about it. Nothing at all.

Asked softly: "What if you're wrong?"

Nick shook his head, though he knew the old man couldn't see it. "If I am wrong, what have we lost? The Anglos come in, they look around, they go away, we're left alone. What have we lost, Dugan?"

Answered softly: "What is ours."

Again the younger man shook his head. This

was an argument as old as he, and older: let more of the world in, it can be done without loss, we have television and radio, for crying out loud; or, keep the world out because it has nothing to do with what makes us what we are.

It was the reason the young were leaving, many of them not coming back.

In a single motion so rapid and smooth it seemed like no motion at all, the old man was on his feet, dusting off his pants, checking the time by the sun. Without speaking he walked to the top of the hill, Nick following to one side and a step behind. When they reached the crest, Dugan pointed to the pale ghost of the moon.

"One more night and it will be done."

Nick said nothing, and the silence spelled his doubt.

"One more night." The old man took his arm; the way down into the valley was slippery and steep. "It takes faith these days, you know." The hint of a smile. "A lot more than it used to, I'm afraid. But it is there."

It wasn't the faith Nick worried about. He had it, too, and even during his time in the outside world, he had kept it.

It wasn't the faith.

It was the killing.

It was what the killing would bring.

SIX

Mulder strolled into his office whistling.

It was the kind of day that began with a gorgeous, unreal sunrise, Hollywood at its best, and carried that promise so well, he was half-afraid he was dreaming. The heat wave had broken three days before, bringing springlike temperatures to the capital, light showers at night to wash the streets, and a steady breeze that had thus far kept pollution from hazing the blue sky.

Leaves weren't dusty, the flowers were bright . . . it was so utterly perfect, it was damn close to sickening.

But he'd take it. He wasn't that much of a fool.

It took a second for him to notice Scully in his chair.

"Morning," he said brightly.

Since the meeting with Skinner, he had resolved two more knots in two more cases that had been bugging him for weeks. For a change, the agents involved were openly and immediately grateful; egos weren't bruised, and two more of the bad guys were on their way to capture.

He also wasn't surprised that Beth Neuhouse, unlike Bournell, hadn't come around to apologize for her behavior. In fact, he hadn't seen her for a week, another sign that life was good and maybe he'd been mistaken about the reprimand setup.

All he needed now was a generous supply of sunflower seeds, and things would be perfect.

"So what's up?" he asked, dropping his briefcase beside an overloaded desk.

Scully reached down beside her, and tossed him a plastic bag.

He caught it against his chest one-handed and held it up. It was a half-pound of sunflower seeds. He smiled. A sign; it had to be a sign. The smile turned to suspicion. "You hate it when I eat these things. It gets messy. You hate messy." He hefted the bag. "What's the catch?"

She shrugged innocently and reached down again, into her own briefcase. She wore a green suit and loose matching blouse fastened at the collar.

"What's the catch, Scully?" he repeated, tossing the bag onto his desk.

She held up a folder, waggled it, and placed it in her lap almost primly.

He stared at the folder, at her, and at the sunflower seeds. They were definitely a sign, and he had no intention of reading it.

Scully smiled faintly at his expression. "Don't worry. You'll probably like this one."

He waited.

She settled back in the chair. "So, what do you know about cattle mutilations?"

"Oh, please, Scully, not that again, please." He crossed to a wheeled office chair and dropped into it, swiveling around to face her as he crossed his legs at the knee. He wasn't going to answer what was obviously a rhetorical question, until he realized he had to. She was preparing him, preparing his mind for something "ordinary" didn't describe.

"All right." He clasped his hands loosely, elbows on the chair's arms. "Depending on who you talk to, you either have half-baked cults that demand bizarre sacrifices—cows being the animal of choice—secret government experiments in immunology based on actual and potential chemical warfare, chemical warfare tests alone, or . . ." He looked at the ceiling. "Or experiments with alleged alien-based technology." He shook his head slowly. "To name a few."

Without responding, she flipped open the folder. "The cattle are either bled, they have sections of hide and/or muscle and/or organs removed—"

"—or they're just sliced all to hell and left in the middle of a field for some poor farmer to fall over. So what? You know this isn't the sort of thing I—" He stopped, and they looked at each other.

He had almost said, "need to know."

He broke contact first, staring at the tip of his shoe. "Where?"

"New Mexico."

He barked a laugh. "Cattle mutilations? Right. Near Roswell, I suppose. Come on, Scully, give me a break. I'm not about to get into that—"

She held up a pair of photographs without comment.

After a moment he took them; after another moment, he placed both feet on the floor and leaned over, elbows now resting on his thighs. It took a while for him to understand what he was looking at, and when he did, he inhaled quickly.

At first they seemed to be little more than solid masses of stained white and gray lying on what appeared to be bare earth. Sandy, grainy, maybe desert ground. A blink to change the perspective, and their forms resolved into the carcasses of animals that had been skinned, stripped in some areas right to the bone. There was virtually nothing left of their heads but exposed skull.

"The one on the left," she told him, "hadn't been found for a couple of days."

Its eyes were gone, and a closer examination showed him swarming ants, and a few flies the photographer hadn't been able to shoo away. Its hind legs had been twisted from their sockets; its mouth was open, the tongue still there, but it was much smaller, thinner than it ought to be, and evidently raw. Although there were shadows, and although he tried, he couldn't spot any pools or traces of blood.

He glanced up, frowning. "Blood?"

Scully nodded. "I know, I've looked, too. If it's exsanguination, it's almost too well done. Otherwise . . ." A one-shoulder shrug. "Cauterization is about the only other thing I can think of. Based on the pictures, that is. To know exactly, we'll have to talk to those who were at the scene."

At her direction, he checked the photograph on the right.

"Now that one," she explained, "was found, they think, only a few hours after it happened. The eyes are gone there as well, but I can't tell if they've been surgically removed or . . ."

She didn't finish; she didn't have to.

"The blood thing again," he said, looking from one exhibit to the other.

"Right. And again, I don't have an answer for you. Not based on what we have now. Look close at the hind quaters, though. Twisted, just like the other one. I doubt if they're still in their sockets. There was a lot of force exerted there, Mulder. A lot."

"Meaning?"

"Too soon, Mulder, you know that. Most of the hide is gone, although—" She leaned over and pointed. "—it looks as if there are still some strips around the belly. Maybe between the legs, too. With all that muscle tisssue gone or shredded, it's hard to tell."

He looked up. "This isn't just skinning. What do you figure? Flayed?"

She nodded cautiously, unwilling as always to commit until she had seen the evidence firsthand. "I think so. I won't know until I've had a good look for myself."

Then she handed him another pair.

Puzzled, he took them, looked down, and rocked back in the chair, swallowing heavily. "Jesus."

People; they were people.

He closed his eyes briefly and set the pictures aside. He had seen any number of horrors over the past several years, from dismemberment to outright butchery, but there had been nothing as vicious as this. He didn't need to look at them more than once to know this was something different. To put it mildly.

Flayed.

These people had been flayed, and he didn't need to ask if they had been alive when it happened.

"Skinner, right?" The Assistant Director would have flagged this for him as soon as it had arrived.

Scully nodded as she pushed absently at her hair, trying to tuck it behind one ear. "The local authorities, the county sheriff's office, called . . ." She checked a page of the file. "They called Red Garson in the Albuquerque office. Apparently it didn't take him very long to think of you."

Mulder knew Garson slightly, a weathered, rangy westerner who had breezed through the Bureau academy at Quantico, less with considerable skill—although he had it in abundance—than with an almost frantic enthusiasm born of a man determined to get out of the East as fast as he could. Which he had done as soon as he could. He was no slouch when it came to on-site investigations, so this must have thrown him completely. It wasn't like him to ask for anyone's help.

"Mulder, whoever did this is truly sick."

Sick, deranged, or so devoid of emotion that he might as well not be human.

He grabbed a picture at random—it was a couple, and he was thankful that what was left of their faces was turned away from the camera.

"Tied? Drugged?"

Scully cleared her throat. "It's hard to tell, but

initial indications are . . ." She paused, and he heard the nervousness, and the anger, in her voice. "Indications are they weren't. And Garson doesn't think they were killed somewhere else and dumped at the site."

He rubbed a hand over his mouth, bit down on his lower lip thoughtfully.

"Autopsies by the medical examiner, a woman named Helen Rios, are inconclusive on whether they were actually conscious or not at the time of death. The lack of substantial quantities of epinephrine seems to indicate it happened too fast for the chemical to form, which it usually does in abundance in cases of extreme violence."

"A victim's adrenaline rush," he said quietly.

Scully looked up from the report. "Right. Something else, too."

He didn't know what question to ask.

"They appear to have been dressed at the time of the assault."

He shifted uneasily. "Wait."

"Shards of clothing were found around each of the scenes. Not even that—no more than bits. Strips of leather from boots or shoes. Metal buttons."

"Scully, hold it."

Her hand trembling slightly, she dropped the folder back into her briefcase. "The pathologist says they either died of shock or bled to death." She inhaled slowly. "Garson, in a sidebar, seems to think they were frightened to death, that they were dead before they hit the ground."

Mulder waved her silent. "Scully, these people—forget about the animals for a minute—these people were attacked by someone, or a group of someones, flayed until their clothes were shredded and their skin was taken off." He gestured vaguely. Shook his head. "You're saying—"

"*They're* saying," she corrected.

"Okay. Okay, they're saying it happened so fast, epinephrine hadn't had time to . . ." He smiled without humor and looked blindly around the room. "Scully, you know as well as I do that's damn near impossible."

"Probably," she admitted. "I haven't had a lot of time to think about it."

He stood abruptly. "You don't have to think about it, Scully. There's nothing to think about. It's practically flat-out impossible."

"Which is why we have to be at Dulles first thing in the morning. Stopover at Dallas, we'll be in New Mexico by one their time." She raised a finger to forestall a response. "And remember: practically is the right word here, Mulder. That does not mean definitely."

He stared at her briefcase, spread his arms at all the work yet undone he could see in the office, and said, "What?" at the twitch of a smile on her lips.

She didn't have to answer.

He usually reacted this way when a clear X-File landed in his lap. A switching of gears, of mind-set, excitement of one kind changing to excitement of another. Impossible, to him, meant someone else had decided there were no explanations for whatever had happened.

But there were always explanations.

Always.

His superiors, and Scully, didn't always like them, but they were there.

Sometimes all it took was a little imagination to find them. A less hidebound way of looking at the world. A willingness to understand that the truth sometimes wore a mask.

"There's something else," she added as he reached for the sunflower seeds and his briefcase.

"What?"

She stood and brushed at her skirt. "There was a witness to one of the killings."

He felt his mouth open. "You're kidding. He saw who did it?"

"She," Scully corrected. "And she claims it wasn't a person."

He waited.

"She said it was a shadow."

Brother, he thought.

"Either that, or a ghost."

SEVEN

A low fire burned in a shallow pit.

Smoke rose in dark trails, winding fire-reflected patterns around the large underground room before escaping through the ragged round hole in the ceiling.

Shadows on the roughly hewn rock walls cast by shadows seated on planks around the pit.

Six men, cross-legged and naked, their bodies lean and rawhide-taut, stringlike hair caught in the sweat that glittered in the firelight, their hands on their knees. Their eyes on the flames that swayed to a breeze not one of them could feel.

Over the fire, resting on a metal grate, a small, flame-blackened pot in which a colorless liquid bubbled without raising steam.

A seventh man sat on a chair carved from dull red stone, back in the shadows where the rite said he belonged. He wore no clothing save a cloth headband embedded with polished stones and gems, none of them alike, none bigger than the tip of a finger. In his right hand he held the spine of a snake; from his left hand dangled the tail of a black horse, knotted at the end and wound through with blue, red, and yellow ribbons. His black eyes were unfocused.

Eventually one of the six stirred, chest rising and falling in a long, silent sigh. He took a clay ladle from the hand of the man on his left, dipped it into the pot, and stood as best he could on scrawny legs that barely held him. A word spoken to the fire. A word spoken to the smoke-touched night sky visible through the hole. Then he carried the ladle to the man in the chair, muttered a few words, and poured the boiling liquid over the seventh man's head.

The man didn't move.

The water burned through his hair, over his shoulders, down his back and chest.

He still didn't move.

The horsetail twitched, but the hand that held it didn't move.

The old man returned to the circle, sat, and after shifting once, didn't move.

The only sound was the fire.

* * *

A lone man waiting in the middle of nowhere.

He stood in the center of a scattering of bones—coyote, mountain lion, horse, bull, ram, snake.

And from where he stood, he could see smoke rising above Sangre Viento Mesa, rising in separate trails until, a hundred feet above, it gathered itself into a single dark column that seemed to make its way to the moon.

In the center of the smoke-made basket the moonlight glowed emerald.

The man smiled, but there was no humor.

He spread his arms as if to entice the smoke toward him.

It didn't move.

He was patient.

It had moved before; it would move again.

And after tonight, when the old fools had finished, he would make it move on his own.

All he had to do was believe.

Donna rolled over in her sleep, moaning so loudly it woke her up. She blinked rapidly to dispel the nightmare, and when she was sure it was done, she swung her legs over the side of the bed and sat up, pushing hair away from her eyes, mouth open to catch the cool air that puckered her skin and made her shiver.

The house was quiet.

The neighborhood, such as it was, was quiet.

Moonlight slipped between the cracks the curtains left over the room's two windows, slants of it that trapped sparkling particles of dust.

She yawned and stood, yawned again as she scratched at her side and under her breasts. The nightmare was gone, scattered, but she knew she had had one, knew it was probably the same one she had had over the past two weeks:

She walked in the desert, wearing only a long T-shirt, bare feet feeling the night cold of the desert floor. A steady wind blew into her face. A full moon so large it seemed about to collide with the Earth, and too many stars to count.

Despite the wind's direction, she could hear something moving close behind her, but whenever she looked back, the night was empty except for her shadow.

It hissed at her.

It scraped toward her.

When she couldn't take it any longer, she woke up, knowing that if she didn't, she was going to die.

She didn't believe in omens, but she couldn't help but wonder.

Now she padded sleepily into the kitchen, opened the refrigerator, and wondered if it was too late, or too early, to have a beer. Not that it mattered. If she had one now, she'd be in the bathroom before dawn, cursing herself and wondering how she'd make it through the day with so little sleep.

She let the door swing shut with a righteous nod, yawned, and moved to the back door.

Her yard was small, ending, like all the other yards scattered along the side road, in a stone-block wall painted the color of the earth. Poplars along the back blocked her view of the other houses even though they were too far away to see even in daylight, unless she was right at the wall.

Suddenly she felt much too alone.

There was no one out there.

She was cut off, and helpless.

The panic rose, and she was helpless to stop it. Running from the room did her no good because she could see nothing from the living room window either—the rosebushes she had spent so much time training to be a hedge fragmented her view of the road, erasing sight of the field across the way.

Trapped; she was trapped.

A small cry followed her to the door. She flung it open and ran onto the stoop, stopping before she flung herself off the steps. Cold concrete made her gasp; cold wind plastered the T-shirt to her chest and stomach.

I am, she decided, moving back into town first thing in the morning.

It was the same vow she made after every nightmare, and it made her smile.

Oh boy, tough broad, she thought sarcastically;

think you're so tough, and a lousy dream makes you a puddle.

She stepped back over the threshold, laughing aloud, but not loud enough that she didn't hear the hissing.

The smoke rose and coiled and swallowed the emerald light.

Mike Ostrand was a little drunk.

Hell, he was a lot drunk, and could barely see the dashboard, much less the interstate. The gray slash of his headlamps blurred and sharpened, making the road swing from side to side as if the car couldn't stay in its proper lane.

This late, though, he didn't much give a damn.

The road from Santa Fe was, aside from occasional rises not quite hills, fairly straight all the way to Bernalillo, and into Albuquerque beyond. Just aim the damn thing and hold onto the wheel. He'd done it hundreds of times.

He hiccuped, belched, and grimaced at the sour taste that rose in his throat, shaking his head sharply as if to fling the taste away.

The radio muttered a little Willie Nelson.

He wiped his eyes with one hand and checked the rearview mirror. Nothing back there but black.

Nothing ahead but more black.

The speedometer topped seventy.

If he were lucky, if he were really lucky, he'd be home by two and asleep by two-ten, assuming he made it as far as the bedroom. Two-five if he couldn't get past the couch.

He laughed, more like a giggle, and rolled down the window when he felt a yawn coming. Drunk or not, he knew enough to understand that cold air blasting the side of his face was infinitely preferable to dozing off and ending up nose-down in a ditch, his head through the windshield.

The air smelled good.

The engine's grumble was steady.

"And so am I," he declared to the road. "Steady as a rock and twice as hard."

Another laugh, another belch.

It had been a good night. No, it had been a great night. Those pinheads in Santa Fe, thinking they knew ahead of the rest of the world what the next artsy trend would be, had decided he was it. Living collages, they called it; the desert genius, they called him.

"My God!" he yelled, half in joy, half in derision.

After a dozen years trying to sell paintings even he couldn't abide, he'd sliced a small cactus in half, glued it to a canvas, added a few tiny bird bones and a couple of beads, called it something or other, and as a lark, brought it north.

They loved it.

They fucking loved it.

He had meant it as a thumbed nose at their pretensions, and they had fallen over themselves trying to buy it.

The wind twisted through the car, tangling his long blond hair, tugging at it, threatening a headache.

Five years later, twenty-five carefully assembled when he was roaring drunk canvases later, his bank account was fat, his home was new, his car was turned in every year, and the women were lined up six to the dozen, just waiting for his living desert fingers to work their magic on them.

It almost made him sick.

It didn't make him stupid.

Trends were little more than fads, and he knew full well that the next season might be his last. Which was why he needed to hole up for a while, work through an even dozen more projects, and get himself out before he ended up like the others—flat broke and saying, "I used to be someone, you know, really, I was," while they cadged another beer from a stranger in a strange bar.

The speedometer topped eighty.

The headache began.

Acid bubbled in his stomach.

The back of his hand scrubbed across his face, and when his vision cleared, he saw something to the right, just beyond the edge of the light.

He frowned as he stared at it, then yelped as

the car followed his stare and angled for the shoulder. The correction was too sharp, and he swung off toward the wide empty median, swung back again, hit the accelerator instead of the brakes, and yelled soundlessly when the right-side tires bit into the earth off the blacktop.

The car shuddered.

He froze—turn into the skid? turn out of the skid?—and watched in horror as the low shrubs and deep ditch charged him and veered away at the last minute, putting him back on the road.

Sweat masked his face.

His bladder demanded immediate relief.

His left hand shook so much he thrust it between his knees and squeezed until it calmed.

"My God," he whispered. "Jesus, man, Jesus."

Twenty-five, he swore to himself; he didn't care if it took until dawn, he wouldn't go faster than twenty-five all the way home.

He wasn't sober, but he sure as hell wasn't as drunk as he had been.

The speedometer reached fifty.

He saw the needle, saw it climb again slowly, and decided it would be all right. Sixty, no more; he'd be home quicker, and that was okay because he was a menace to himself out here.

A hard swallow, a deep breath, his right hand flicking the radio off because what he didn't need now was interference with his concentration. Just watch the road, pay no attention to anything that—

He saw it again.

Just a suggestion of movement running with him on the other side of the ditch. Which was impossible. He was doing sixty-five, for God's sake, there wasn't anything except another car that could go that fast.

He squinted a stare, broke it off when the car began to drift, and licked his lips.

There wasn't anything over there.

Good God, there couldn't be anything over there. It was the headlights, that's all, running along a row of juniper maybe, or some piñon, rock, something like that. His eyes caught the strobelike reflection, and the scotch turned it into something that paced him.

That's all it was.

He wished the moon were a little brighter.

Forget the new canvases, he decided a half-mile later; the hell with it, he was done. He had enough money, the house was paid for, what the hell more could he want?

The car jumped sideways when something slammed into the passenger door.

He yelled, and watched his hands blur around the wheel, watched the road blur black to gray and black again, screamed when the car was struck a second time, and looked over to see what drunken idiot was trying to run him off the road.

There was nothing there.

When he looked back, it was too late.

The highway was gone.

All he could do was cross his arms in front of his face, close his eyes, and scream.

There was no fire, no explosion.

Mike Ostrand hung upside down in his seat-belt, listening to the engine tick, listening to the wind blow through the open window.

Listening to the hiss he thought was the tires spinning to a halt.

A few seconds later, he blacked out when something reached through the window and touched his arm.

EIGHT

X La Mosca Inn sat between the Rio Grande and a high adobe wall that fronted the road. Eight units extended left and right from a central two-story building that housed the office, a large flagstone waiting room cooled by a small sparking fountain, and a restaurant large enough to seat one hundred without elbows and voices clashing. Spanish tile on the roof, shade provided by cottonwood and mountain ash, and a single huge Russian olive in the center of the courtyard.

Scully sat on a wood bench that ringed the massive tree, facing the arched entrance whose elaborate iron gates were closed each night at, the proprietor told her, precisely midnight. She let her eyes close, and touched a finger to her forehead, to trap a droplet of sweat that had broken from her hairline.

"Feeling better?" a voice rasped beside her.

"Not really."

The day had gone wrong from minute one: she'd overslept and had to race to the airport, only to learn that the flight had been delayed. For an hour. Then two. Once airborne, she had planned to set up her laptop computer, so she and Mulder could go over what details of the case they had.

It didn't happen.

Roller-coaster turbulence rode them all the way to Dallas, making reading the computer screen a nauseating experience; she spent most of the time trying, and failing, to doze. Then a series of thunderstorms ringing the Texas city forced them to swerve wide into a holding pattern until the squall line had passed. Another hour lost, and so was their connecting flight.

"Cursed," Mulder had said at one point. "This whole thing is cursed."

By the time they landed in Albuquerque, she was ready to believe in curses; by the time Red Garson had sped them in his Jeep out of the city, north to Bernalillo, she was ready to spend the rest of her life walking.

The man beside her shifted to get her attention.

She opened her eyes and smiled at him wanly.

Red was as Mulder had told her, a tall, lean, middle-aged man whose lined face and hands spoke of time spent in the mountains and the desert. She had no idea where he'd gotten his nickname, because his blond hair was pale, his blue eyes dark; part of his left ear was missing, bitten off, he told her, in a fight with a man who had a strong aversion to spending the rest of his life in federal prison.

Hardly a stereotypical FBI agent.

When he smiled, only his lips moved; he never showed his teeth.

He jerked his thumb over his shoulder. "You think he's fallen asleep?"

"I doubt it."

A pickup chugged past the Inn, backfired twice, and left a curl of black smoke behind.

"Dana?"

She nodded to show him she was listening.

"Why does he call you Scully all the time? I mean, you do have a first name."

"Because he can," she answered simply, without sarcasm, and didn't bother to explain. Just as it would be hard to explain why Mulder was, without question, the best friend she had. It was more than just being partners, being able to rely on each other when one of them was in danger, or when one of them needed a boost when a case seemed to be going bad; and it was more than simply their contrasting styles, which, perversely to some, complemented each other perfectly.

What it was, she sometimes thought, was an indefinable instinct, a silent signal that let her know that whatever else changed, whatever else happened, Mulder would always be there when he had to be. One way or another.

At that moment she heard a footfall and grinned. "Here he comes."

Garson looked startled, looked around and saw him walking along one of the stone paths that wound through the courtyard garden. She had to admit he looked strange without his suit. Over his shoulder he carried a denim jacket, not for appearance but to hide the holster he wore on his left hip.

He also looked as frazzled as she felt.

"It's hot," he said, dropping onto the bench beside her.

"It's July, Mulder," Garson reminded him. "It's New Mexico. What did you expect?"

"Heat I can get at home. An oven I already have in my apartment." He scratched through his hair and shook his head as though trying to force himself awake.

"It isn't for everybody," Garson admitted, adding without saying so that "everybody" must be crazy if they didn't instantly fall in love with this part of the country. "And remember, you're a mile farther up than you were in Washington.

Thinner air. Take it easy for a while, understand? You go shooting off in fourteen directions at once, you're going to drop."

Mulder grunted, then stood again. "Hey, look." He headed for the gate.

"Mulder," Scully called. "We haven't time—"

He turned, grinning, and pointed to a small dust devil spinning lazily in the road. "We used to get these things at home. Leaves, you know?" He moved closer; it was no higher than his shin. "We'd try to get inside." His foot inched toward the dervish's base and apparently broke some unseen barrier. The dust devil fell apart, and Mulder toed the place where it had been.

Scully, who was already feeling the effects of the altitude, let the silence settle for a few seconds before she said, "Mulder, come over here, I think we'd better not waste any more time." She checked her watch; it was just after four. "I suppose it's too late to catch Dr. Rios. What about . . . Patty? Patty Deven. Is she well enough to talk to us?"

Garson stabbed a thumb at her as Mulder rejoined them. "She always like this?"

"We have three people murdered, Red. The altitude didn't kill them."

The man nodded, accepting the point and the rebuke without taking offense. "The Devens live about a mile down the road. They're fixing to head back to Chicago as soon as this is cleared up.

I'll take you over, but I'm telling you now that you won't be welcome."

He was right.

Scully caught the instant hostility as soon as Kurt Deven opened the trailer door and saw who it was. When Garson introduced his companions, the man scowled and told them to wait. Then he closed the door. Hard.

Mulder nodded toward the riverline of cottonwood sixty or seventy yards away. "Down there?"

"Yep. The bank slopes sharp right about where you're looking. It happened a little ways to the right."

Scully shaded her eyes against the low-hanging sun and tried to see it at night, with little but moon and stars for illumination. The trailer wouldn't help; it was too far away, and except for the skeleton of an unfinished house beside it, there were no other homes in the immediate area, even though she saw flagged wooden stakes in the ground, marking other lots soon to be developed. The nearest trailer was a good sixty yards away.

The door opened.

The two men stepped aside as a woman stepped down onto the cinder-block steps. She was short and slight, with straight blonde hair that needed a brushing, and a lost, empty look in her eyes. When she spoke, rage and grief made her hoarse:

"She doesn't want to talk to you again, Mr. Garson."

Red told her softly he understood, and apologized for the intrusion. "But I have these folks here, Mrs. Deven. All the way from Washington." He cleared his throat, glanced at the open doorway. "They're experts in this kind of crime. If anyone can catch the—"

"Nobody has," she snapped. "It's been two weeks, and nobody has."

Scully lifted a hand to draw her attention. "Mrs. Deven?"

The woman took her time: "What?"

Scully kept her voice gentle. "Mrs. Deven, I won't lie to you. I won't pretend to know how you feel for your loss, or how your daughter feels. But Agent Mulder and I have done this more times than I ever want to tell you. And if nothing else, I can promise you that we don't quit. We're not perfect, but we do not quit."

Mary Deven's hands pressed lightly to her stomach, eyes narrowed. "Are you promising me you'll catch him?"

"No," Mulder answered, just as gently, just as firmly. "We're only promising you that we won't quit. And if you don't want us to bother you, or your family, you won't have to worry."

Mrs. Deven stared at the trees, blinking rapidly,

then not at all. "Just don't take her down there," she said, barely above a whisper. "You take her down there, I'll lose her."

Scully agreed readily, and said nothing when Mulder asked Garson to show him the scene. After all this time, there wouldn't be anything left of real value—Garson and his men and the local police would have raked it over thoroughly. Mulder, however, had a knack for finding things in barren places, a knack she didn't pretend to understand as well as she wanted to.

"Agent Scully?"

Wan, painfully thin, Patty Deven was the mirror image of her mother, right down to the haunted look. A fading bruise spread across her right cheek and temple. Her eyes were too large behind her glasses.

They sat on two lawn chairs. There was no shade, and no offer of a drink.

After a long silence, with the girl staring at the knot of fingers in her lap, Scully leaned forward and said, "What did you see, Patty?" Nothing more.

Mulder stood on the bare ground, checked the branches above him, glanced at the shallow river below. "Here?"

"Just about," Garson said.

But "here" was nothing. The ground was too hard for tracks, and with no direct line of sight to the trailer, there was nothing much to work on. He asked Garson to stand approximately where Patty had been, and scowled.

Dark night, thirty or forty feet away, she wouldn't have been able to see much of anything.

Flashes of movement that accompanied her brother's attack and screams.

She saw a ghost because there was nothing true to focus on.

He hunkered down and ran a palm over the ground. "Have you had rain?"

Garson walked back, taking his time. "This is what we call the monsoon season, Mulder. You wouldn't know to look at it now, but afternoons we get storms in. Big ones. Usually from the west, and they don't fool around." He shrugged as Mulder stood. "Trouble is, rain washes the evidence away, and the ground's like rock again before noon the next day. This is a waste of time."

Maybe, Mulder thought; maybe not.

He walked north along the bank, gaze shifting slowly from side to side. Ahead, the underbrush was thick, still uncleared by the developers. He saw no signs that anyone had broken through, which meant they had either come from down below, or from the far side of the trees.

It was something, and it was nothing.

By the time he reached the other agent, he was scowling again. "Gangs?"

"Some." They headed back to the trailer. "This is no gang hit, though. Knives and guns; nothing like this."

"Cults?"

They left the trees behind, and he felt the temperature already beginning to rise. Scully was still in her lawn chair; she was alone.

"What kind of cults you want, Mulder? We have New Age swamis communing in the desert. We have the Second Coming believers who wander around the mountains and then use their cellulars when they get lost. And we have the flying saucer nuts, who figure Roswell is the key to all intergalactic understanding." A sideways glance Mulder didn't miss. "That's kind of your territory, isn't it?"

The only answer was a noncommittal grunt, and Garson was smart enough to leave it alone.

Scully stood as they approached, a brief shake of her head when he looked her a question. At that moment he couldn't help a yawn, and turned away so the pale face in the trailer window couldn't see him.

He hoped he had been quick enough.

The one thing Mary Deven didn't need now was the sight of an FBI agent yawning at the site of her only son's murder.

Garson saw it, though. "We're going back," he told them both, not giving them an option to refuse. "You two get something to eat and get some sleep, or you're going to be worthless tomorrow."

"Why? What's tomorrow?"

He touched his hat brim. "Tomorrow, my friend, you're going to meet a genuine movie star."

NINE

Mulder couldn't sleep.

After a slow, almost lethargic dinner, he listened as Scully told him about the interview with the girl, which hadn't told her anything new. Patty had seen even less than her statement had implied. Almost as soon as the attack began, the branch club her brother had been holding spiraled out of the dark and struck her on the side of the face. She had fallen, dazed, and in that state thought she might have heard someone whispering, someone else laughing.

But it was all too muddled, and she had passed out shortly afterward.

It was her father who had found the body.

"No ghosts, Scully," Mulder had said, walking her back to her room. "We're dealing with people here."

"You sound disappointed."

He hadn't answered then, and he had no answer now as he put on a jacket and left the room, glad now that he had listened to Garson—despite the day's heat, the desert was downright cold at night.

He walked through a short passageway between the rooms and the main building, and paused.

The back was a garden of cacti and now-closed desert flowers set in random circles ringed by stone, as it was in front. Stone paths wound between them and joined at the back to lead to a half-dozen benches that faced the river. Cottonwoods and willows were illuminated by miniature lanterns hanging amid their leaves, leaving patches of lazy shifting light on the ground.

He wasn't sure, but he thought he smelled honeysuckle.

When he was sure he was alone, he sat on one of the benches and watched what little water there was flow past his feet, electric lanterns on metal riverbank poles glowing just enough to turn the dark to gray.

The moon was out.

He shoved his hands into his jacket pockets and watched it for a while, thinking of nothing in particular until a slip of a cloud gave the moon a face.

Patty Deven, or her mother, adrift in a darkness they would never be able to escape. Pale, only shadows for expression, only hints of what used to be behind their smiles.

It was an all too easy, and all too painful, jump from there to his sister, gone too many years now. Taken when she was eight, by someone, or something, hiding behind the glare of a light that even now he couldn't think about without shuddering, or squinting to shut it out.

To try to see what was behind it.

That was the foundation of his pursuit of the truths buried somewhere within the X-Files.

He looked away from the moon and wiped a hand over his face, then absently rubbed the back of his neck.

He would find Samantha, there was no question about it; until then, however, the best he could do would be to find the men who had murdered Patty's brother.

Again his hand passed over his face. When it slipped into its jacket pocket, though, a brief smile was left behind.

"I'm okay," he said, shifting over to make room for Scully. "Just thinking."

"Out here, that'll get you pneumonia."

"Is that a doctor's truth thing?"

She stretched out her legs, folded her hands on

her stomach. "No, it's cold, that's what it is. God, Mulder, why can't you ever have a mood someplace warm?"

They said nothing else for a long time, watching the river, listening to the rustle of the trees, once in a while listening to a dog bark or a car roar past the Inn. For a while the garden filled with diners having after-dinner drinks as they strolled among the garden islands, conversation soft, laughter sometimes loud; for a while the evening breeze stopped, and they couldn't hear a thing but their own breathing.

Then Mulder said, "Scully, has it occurred to you that maybe the people who mutilated those cows weren't the ones who killed Patty's brother and that couple?"

"No," she said at last. She looked over. "Why?"

"The history, Scully, the history. Animal mutilations of this sort aren't usually tied to murder. Particularly not brutal ones like these. The animals are assaulted, not people."

He watched her carefully as she looked away. He'd only been thinking aloud, but once the thought had been voiced, he had to make sure.

"No," she repeated with a slow shake of her head. "Whatever was used, however it was done, the timing's too close, the similarities too great. From what we've been told." She shifted uneasily. "I'll know more when I speak to the M.E., but . . ." She shook her head again. "No." A quick smile.

"Besides, aren't you the one who told me that there are coincidences, and then there are coincidences? One is real, the other only an illusion?"

He returned the smile. "Yep."

"Okay. Well, this is no real coincidence, Mulder. The brutality itself is a strong indication of that. All we need to do is find the connection."

"Right. All we need to do."

"Then think about this, Scully," he said quietly. "Why? What's so damn important out here that both cattle *and* kids have to die?"

She didn't respond; he hadn't expected her to.

But he had a strong feeling, an unpleasant one, that whatever answer they finally uncovered, it would be one neither of them would like.

In the middle of the desert, they had been dropped into a nightmare.

"I am not crazy!" Mike Ostrand insisted from his hospital bed. He glared at Sheriff Sparrow, who returned the look without expression. "I did not imagine the accident. I did not imagine this goddamn cast on my goddamn arm. I did not imagine my brand-new car flipped over and left me hanging there like a goddamn Peking duck!"

Sparrow was patient.

"Okay." Ostrand shifted uncomfortably, lips pulling away from his teeth in a grimace. "Okay.

So I was a little drunk, I admit it. But that's not why I crashed."

"No, you crashed because some kind of mysterious vehicle, so low you couldn't see it out your window, deliberately forced you off the road."

Ostrand looked at him angrily. "That's right."

"And then it tried to kill you when you were hanging from your seatbelt."

The artist shrugged, winced at the pain that exploded in his shoulder, and sighed capitulation. "Okay, okay, so it was a stupid coyote, okay? So I was so damn scared it scared the hell out of me. It would have scared anybody. But it wasn't a coyote that ran me off the damn road!"

"Good." Sparrow nodded sharply. "Now we're getting somewhere." He glanced down at the small notepad he held in his left hand, chewed on the eraser end of his pencil for a moment, and said, "Now, about that invisible vehicle . . ."

The Coronado Bar was unoriginal in both name and decor. As Bernalillo inexorably changed from an outpost on the Rio Grande into an Albuquerque bedroom community, the Coronado just as stubbornly refused to change with it. A long bar on the right-hand wall, tables and booths everywhere else, and a jukebox that muttered country-western all day long. The TV on the wall in back never played anything but sports, minor league baseball tonight from Southern California. Smoke and liquor in the air, as many cigarette butts on the bare floor as in the aluminum ashtrays. It catered neither to the tourists nor the newcomers, and didn't much care that business didn't boom. It did well enough, which was well enough for its regulars.

Indian Territory was at the back.

Although there were a handful of exceptions, most of the men who drove in from the pueblos stuck to the two last booths and three last tables. There was nothing belligerent about it; it just happened that way. Even the Spanish stayed away.

Especially when the Konochine came to town.

Leon Ciola nursed a long-neck beer in the last booth. He was alone, seated under a wall lamp whose bulb he had unscrewed as soon as he'd taken his seat. He didn't like the light, didn't like the way the Anglos tried not to stare at the web of scars across his face or the scars on his knuckles.

It was better to sit in shadow.

It was also better to face the entrance, so when the man came in, Ciola would see him first and lift a hand in greeting, before a question could be asked or a voice raised. What he didn't need tonight was talk, debate—*What's the matter with your people, Leon, don't they believe in the twentieth century?* The time for that was past. The others— Nick Lanaya, Dugan Velador, fools like that—

they could do their best to keep the talk alive, to deal with Anglo crooks like that Falkner woman and sell the People down the river without an ounce of guilt. Not him. He had plans.

They thought he was beaten. They thought his time away would change him.

He drank, not sipped.

It had.

It had changed him.

It had made him worse.

Just before eleven the man came in, spotted him right away, and dropped heavily into the booth.

Ciola tugged on the beak on his cap, a greeting and an adjustment. "You're late."

"Shit truck wouldn't start. Wasn't for you, I wouldn't make the effort."

Ciola watched him, hiding his distaste by emptying the bottle and waving it over his head, so the waitress, such as she was, would bring him another.

The other man didn't ask for one, and one wasn't offered.

"So?" Leon said.

The man lifted one shoulder. "So they brought in some FBI, straight from Washington. They came in this morning. One man, one woman."

Ciola coughed a laugh. "You're kidding."

"They're supposed to be experts."

"A woman?"

The man nodded, and offered a lopsided grin. "Gets better. They're Anglos."

The empty bottle was taken away, a full one left in its place. The man grabbed it before Ciola did, took a long swallow, and set it down. His fingers stayed around the neck. "Am I worried?"

"No."

"Good." The man stood and hitched up his pants. "I hate being worried. It always pisses me off."

He left without a word to anyone else.

The bartender turned up the baseball game.

Ciola wiped the bottle's mouth with his palm and drank the rest without coming up for air.

When the waitress returned for the empty, he grabbed her wrist, just strongly enough to keep her bent over the table. "*Chica,*" he said softly, "what are you doing tonight?"

"Getting a life," she answered, yanking her arm free. "Try it sometime."

He laughed. Not a sound, but he tilted his head back and laughed. Wonderful! She was wonderful! He wiped a tear from his eye and shook his head. Since she didn't want him, he would leave her the biggest tip she had ever had in her miserable life.

And to make it better, he wouldn't even kill her.

Scully massaged the back of her neck. It was hard to keep her eyes open, and she didn't bother to hide a yawn.

"The desert night air," Mulder said. "It's almost too peaceful here."

"I know." She dropped her hand into her lap. "The point is, Mulder, we haven't enough data yet to show us why they were killed, much less explain the connections in any reasonable fashion. And I don't think we're going to find them out here. Not tonight, anyway." She smiled wanly. "I think I'm a little too punchy."

"We both are." He stretched one arm at a time over his head, clasped his hands, and pushed his palms toward the sky. "I just wish I could see the connections between a handful of cows, a kid by the river, and a couple in the desert." He brought his arms down, one hand again moving to his nape.

"Mulder, relax, we just got here, remember? Besides, you have to remember that the thinner air out here slows down the intellectual process, the result of less oxygen flowing to the brain."

He grinned and looked at her sideways. "Is that a doctor thing?"

"No, that's a Scully thing." She grinned and pushed off the bench and held out her hand. When he grabbed it, she pulled him up, turned him around, pushing him lightly toward the motel. "The doctor thing is, get some sleep, like Red said, or you'll be useless in the morning."

He nodded as he waved a weary good night over his shoulder, sidestepping a garden wall just before he tripped over it. Another wave—*I'm okay, I know what I'm doing*—before he disappeared into the passageway, and she couldn't help wondering what it was like for him—seeing things other people sometimes couldn't; engaging in a pursuit with oftentimes terrifying intensity; looking so young and deceptively guileless that there had been many times when he was severely underestimated.

She wasn't surprised when, passing his room on her way to bed, she saw light slipping around the edges of the drapes.

Exhausted or not, he would be up most of the night, turning over what he knew, and setting up what he didn't know so he would know the right questions to ask, beyond the how and who and why.

She wished him luck.

Right now, she was having difficulty remembering her own name.

She fingered her key out of her pocket, moved on to the next room . . . and stopped as she inserted the key in the lock.

You're tired, Dana, that's all.

She looked anyway.

The Inn gates were closed, the lanterns out. Only a faint glow from a nearby streetlamp reached over the wall.

A man stood at the gate, arms loose at his sides.

She couldn't see his face or his clothes; just his outline.

Tired, she reminded herself, and pushed into

the room, flicked on the wall switch, and, as she closed the door, checked the gate again.

He was still there.

Watching.

TEN

Mulder didn't have to be outside to know it was hot and getting hotter, even though it was just past ten. Even with sunglasses, the sun's glare was almost too much, and to stare at the passing scenery too long made it jump and shimmer, showing him things he knew weren't there.

There were no clouds, no signs of rain. It was hard to believe there ever was.

He rode with Scully in the back seat of Sheriff Sparrow's dusty blue-and-white cruiser, Garson up front on the passenger side. It was evident from their conversation that the two men had known each other for a long time, using shorthand gestures and single-word answers, mostly grunts. As far as Mulder could tell, the gist of it was, there had been no further incidents since the death of the boy, except for a drunk driver who claimed to have been forced off the road by an invisible, or incredibly short, vehicle.

"It brings out the nuts, this kind of thing," the sheriff said, lifting his gaze to the rearview mirror. "You find that, too, Agent Mulder?"

He nodded. It was true. Just as it was true that Chuck Sparrow was laying on the western sheriff routine a little thick, constantly hitching his gunbelt, chewing a wad of gum that was supposed to simulate tobacco, getting a deeper drawl in his voice every time he opened his mouth. It wasn't necessarily a bad thing, but it made him wonder why the act at all. Garson would have already filled the man in, and it was the sheriff who had finally asked the FBI for help.

It didn't sit right.

Like not wearing a suit and tie, like wearing running shoes.

He knew Garson was right—wearing his usual clothes out here would have been ludicrous as well as stupid; still, like the sheriff, it didn't sit right.

The Sandias passed them on the right as Interstate 25 left the Albuquerque suburbs behind. And although other ranges broke the horizon, there was nothing out there now but the high desert.

And the sun.

"Cult," Sparrow said then, raising his voice to be heard over the air conditioning.

"What?" Scully, startled out of a reverie, asked him to repeat it.

"Cult. You know . . . cult. One of them Satanist things, probably. Look hard enough, betcha them poor folks were all involved somehow."

"A seventeen-year-old boy?" Mulder asked skeptically.

"Hey, that ain't no rare thing, you know what I mean? You got your heavy-metal crap with all that subliminal stuff, you got your rap stuff telling kids to kill cops, shit like that . . . drugs and sex . . ." He lifted a hand off the wheel, palm up. "What more do you want?"

Mulder saw his eyes in the mirror, watching him, gauging.

"Maybe," he answered reluctantly.

"No maybe about it, son, no maybe about it."

Fifteen miles later, at a speed Mulder thought would soon launch them into orbit, the cruiser slowed, pulled onto the right shoulder, and crossed a narrow wooden bridge. A two-lane paved road led into the desert.

Sparrow pointed with a thumb. "What you got up there, them hills there about ten miles along, is what they call the Konochine Wall." He scratched under his hat. "Kind of like a jagged outline of a lightbulb lying on its side. Fat part, it's pointing toward the Sandias back there to the south. The base part, it crosses the road onto the ranch where we're going. Unless you want to climb the hills, the only way in or out is a gap where the road is."

Mulder watched a barbed-wire fence blur past on his left. Beyond it was desert, and he couldn't imagine how anyone could raise anything out here, much less cattle. When he had asked at breakfast, Garson only told him to hold onto his horses, he didn't want to spoil the surprise.

"Do the Konochine fit in here?" Scully asked. "This case, I mean."

Sparrow shrugged one broad shoulder. "Who the hell knows? Doubt it myself. Their place isn't like the other pueblos, see. It's a res and all, but they don't like tourists, they don't like Anglos, they don't like other Indians . . ." He laughed. "Hell, I don't think they much like each other a whole hell of a lot." He yanked at an earlobe, then scratched vigorously behind it. "Some of them, mostly the young ones, they've been trying for years to change things. Most of the time it don't work, though, and they leave, don't come back."

"And the ones who do?"

"Well . . ." He glanced at Garson. "Nick Lanaya, right?"

Garson nodded agreement and half-turned so he wouldn't have to yell. "Nick's a good guy. He went off to college, and came back with enough ideas to fill a canyon. Because of his family, he's on the Tribal Council, so he has to be heard. And he is, believe me. Trouble is, not a lot are listening."

"So why does he stay?"

Garson thought a moment before saying, "Because they're his people."

Sparrow chuckled, sarcasm, not humor. "Doesn't hurt he's making a few bucks, Red."

Garson sighed dramatically, a wink at Mulder to signal what was obviously a long-standing argument. "Nick," he explained, "has a deal with a local woman, an Anglo, Donna Falkner. He brings out some of the crafts the Konochine make, she sells them in town or up in Santa Fe, they each get a cut and the tribe gets the rest. Mostly jewelry," he added. "Once in a while some incredible bowls and ceremonial-style plates, things like that. Every time he brings out a load, he has a fight with the other side, who claim he's selling their heritage down the river."

"And every time he brings back the bucks to the Mesa," Sparrow said sourly, "they line up with their goddamn hands out."

"The mesa?" Scully said.

"Sangre Viento Mesa," Garson explained. "It's in

the middle of the reservation. Their homes are at the base, their religious ceremonies are held up top."

"What does that mean, Sangre Viento?"

Garson faced front. "Blood Wind. It means Blood Wind."

Eventually the barbed wire gave way to a short stretch of well-maintained split rail. In its center was an open gate over which was a wide wood arch. Burned into the face was *Double-H*.

Mulder sat up as Sparrow drove under the arch, onto a hard-ground road. He looked between the men in front and saw what surely had to be a mirage:

A wide expanse of impossibly green grass inside a blinding white fence; a long adobe and Spanish tile ranch house so simple in its design it looked prohibitively expensive; a stable and corral behind and to the left, with a small black horse plodding toward the shade of a tree he couldn't name; a two-car garage behind and to the right, the driveway curving around the fence to join the entrance road in front; *ristras*—strings of dried red chiles—hanging from vigas protruding from the walls beneath a porch that had to be fifty or sixty feet long.

"You want to be a millionaire and live like this, Scully?"

"I wouldn't mind."

Sparrow parked in a cleared patch of ground beside the driveway, took off his hat and slicked his hair back. He opened the door, and paused as he leaned forward to slide out.

"I would appreciate it," he told them, "if you wouldn't bother her too much. She only found the bodies. She didn't see anything else."

From that unsubtle warning, Mulder fully expected a withered and frail woman to greet them, not the beautiful woman who came out of the double front doors and stood on the porch, shading her eyes and smiling.

Scully joined him while Sparrow fumbled with the gate latch, and as they approached the porch, a man and woman stepped out of the house and moved to one side, she in a simple white dress, he in work clothes. Their expressions were anything but friendly.

"Hey, Annie," the sheriff called, and when they were close enough, he made the introductions.

Ann Hatch, Mulder thought as he shook her cool dry hand and looked down into those incredibly green eyes; so this is Ann Hatch.

As she waved them to seats around a wrought-iron table, it was clear Scully liked her at first sight. "You know," she said, accepting a tall glass of lemonade from the woman in white, "this is like finding an oasis, it's so lovely."

Annie's eyes widened in pleasant surprise. "Why, thank you. But it's just my home."

She smiled broadly, and ten minutes later, the three of them were chatting as if they were old friends, long separated but never far from mind. Mulder didn't believe for a minute she was acting.

Another ten minutes passed before he sat back, abruptly sobered when she noted but didn't remark on the holster at his hip. She caught the change in his mood instantly, and took a deep breath.

"You want to know what I saw, and how."

"If you don't mind, Mrs. Hatch."

She rolled her eyes. "Oh, for God's sake, Agent Mulder, please call me Annie. And I don't mind at all." Her gaze shifted to the improbable lawn and the desert beyond it. "They were newlyweds, you know. They were on their honeymoon."

He knew; he had read the report so many times, he could have recited it word for word, footnote for footnote.

Doris and Matt Constella, from Kansas, twenty-five, in Albuquerque only four days, and, from all Garson could figure out, on a wandering drive around the county in a rented van. They had already stopped to visit at least two of the pueblos, and it was there, it was supposed, they had heard about the Konochine. There was no other reason why they'd be on that road. There were no signs, not for the road itself, and not for the ranch.

She explained how she had discovered their bodies, and how she had immediately ridden back to call the sheriff. "Near the gap," she said sadly. "They were right by the gap."

So much for the connection between them and the boy, Mulder thought.

"Mrs. Hatch," Scully began, and cut herself off at the woman's chiding look. "Annie. Have you had any trouble with people from the reservation?"

Annie blinked once, slowly. "No."

She's lying, Mulder thought, and looked to his left when he sensed movement. Nando Quintodo had taken a short step forward, one of his hands fisted at his side. When he saw Mulder look, however, he stopped, his face bland, his hand quickly relaxed.

"Why do you ask?" Annie said.

"It's routine," Mulder answered before Scully, and grinned at her skepticism. "I know, it sounds like a line from a movie, but it's true. We've been told there's some trouble, and . . ." An apologetic gesture. "We can't afford not to ask."

Scully echoed the procedure, and apologized as she took Annie through her story again. Mulder, meanwhile, stretching as if he were too stiff to sit, rose with a muttered apology and left the table. As soon as he took a step, Quintodo walked away from him, heading for the door.

Mulder spoke his name.

When the man turned, his hand was a fist again.

Mulder leaned against the porch rail and looked out over the lawn. He didn't raise his voice; he knew the man could hear him. "Tourists ever call you Tonto?"

"Not here. No tourists here." Flat, unemotional. Careful.

"But sometimes."

There was a pause.

Mulder waited.

"Yes. In town. Sometimes." Still flat, still unemotional.

Mulder faced him, leaning back against the rail, one hand in his pocket. "You're from . . .?"

Quintodo's eyes shifted to the table, shifted back. "The Mesa."

"Your wife, too?"

He nodded.

"So tell me, Mr. Quintodo. Why would a woman like that want to lie?"

The sheriff, mumbling something to Annie, stood.

Quintodo saw him, and Mulder couldn't miss the flare of hatred in his eyes.

"Why?" he repeated softly.

But Sparrow was already on his way over, a mirthless grin beneath dark glasses. "Why what?" he asked, rubbing a hand over his chest.

"Why would I want to visit the stable when I don't ride?" Mulder answered. "I'll tell you why—because I'm a city boy, and I'd like to be able to see manure firsthand."

"Very well, Mr. Mulder," Quintodo agreed before the sheriff could say anything. "I will show you everything. Mrs. Hatch, she has a pair of very fine horses. I think you will be impressed. Maybe you will learn something."

He nodded politely to Sparrow and went inside without looking back.

The sheriff hitched up his belt, and spat over the railing. "This is a beautiful place."

"Yes, it is."

"Annie's been alone out here for a long time, you know. Some say too long."

"I wouldn't know, Sheriff."

Sparrow spat again. "Let me give you some advice, Agent Mulder."

"Always ready to listen, Sheriff Sparrow. You're the expert around here, not me."

Sparrow nodded sharply, *damn right.*

"Okay, number one is, Nando there is a Konochine. You know that already, I assume. Don't trust him. He may live out here with Annie, but his heart's still over the Wall."

Mulder said nothing.

"Second thing is . . ." He stopped. He took off his hat, wiped sweat from his brow with a forearm, and shook his head as he walked back to the table.

Mulder watched him.

The second thing, unspoken, was a threat.

ELEVEN

The stable was gloomy, despite the open door. There were six stalls on either side, but most of them hadn't been used in a long time. A scattering of hay on the floor. Tack hung from pegs on the walls. When Mulder looked outside, all he could see was white light; the corral and the black horse were little more than ghosts.

Quintodo stood beside a chestnut, running a stiff brush over its flank. He hadn't looked up when Mulder walked in, didn't give a sign when Scully followed, unsure why Mulder had asked her to meet him out here.

Quintodo concentrated on his grooming. "You know what *tonto* means, Mr. Mulder?"

"My Spanish is—" A deprecating smile. "Lousy."

"Stupid," the man said, smoothing a palm over the horse's rump. "It means stupid." He reached into his hip pocket and pulled out a lump of sugar, handed it to Scully. "She won't bite. Just keep your hand flat, she won't take your fingers."

Scully offered the treat, and the horse snorted and snapped it up, then nuzzled her for more.

"She's a pig," Quintodo said, with a hint of smile. "She'll eat all you give her, then get sick." A loving pat to the animal's side. "Tonto."

With a look, Scully asked Mulder why they were here; he nodded a *be patient*, and put his back to the door. All he said was, "Why?"

Quintodo worked for several long seconds without speaking, the scrape of the brush the only sound. Then:

"She is one, you know."

Mulder's head tilted slightly.

"Konochine. One of us. Her husband, Mr. Hatch, he met her in Old Town, in Albuquerque. She was fifteen, he was from Los Angeles. I don't know what they call it, looking for places to make a movie."

"Scouting," Scully said.

He nodded. "Yes, *gracias*. He told her about the movies, about being in them." The smile finally broke. "All hell broke loose on the Mesa. But he was very persuasive, Mr. Hatch was. Very handsome, very kind. Very young and . . ." He hesitated. "Dreamy. Before we knew it, she was gone. Making movies. Getting married." He looked at Mulder over the horse's back. "They were very happy. Always."

The smile slipped away.

"No children?" Scully asked.

"Not to be."

The horse stamped impatiently, and Quintodo murmured at it before resuming his grooming.

"She is special, Mr. Mulder," he said at last. "She hears the wind."

Scully opened her mouth to question him, and Mulder shook his head quickly.

Quintodo swallowed, second thoughts making him pause.

When he did speak again, he spoke slowly.

"We have priests, you know." The horse stamped again; a fly buzzed in the stifling heat. "Not the Catholic ones, the padres. Konochine got rid of them a long time ago. Our own. Seven, all the time. They . . . do things for us. *Comprende?* You understand? Today they are all men. It happens. Sometimes there are women, but not now. Priests are not . . ." He frowned, then scowled when he couldn't find the word. "They live like us, and then they die. When one dies, there is a ceremonial, and the dead one is replaced."

A two-tone whistle outside interrupted him. Mulder heard hoofbeats trot across the corral.

The chestnut didn't move.

"They know their call," Quintodo explained. "That was for Diamond."

"And the ceremonial?" Mulder prodded quietly.

Quintodo lowered his head, thinking.

"There was one now. Like the others, it lasted six days. No one is allowed to see it. But the wind . . . the wind carries the ceremony to the four corners. Sometimes you can hear it. It talks to itself. It carries the talk from the kiva. The songs. Prayers. Mrs. Hatch . . ." He inhaled slowly, deeply, and looked up at Mulder. "Sometimes you think you hear voices on the wind, yes? You think it's your imagination, no?" He shook his head. "No. But only some, like the kiva priests, can understand. Mrs. Hatch too can understand. We knew this recently, Silvia and I, we could tell because Mrs. Hatch was very nervous, very . . ." He gestured helplessly.

"Afraid?" Scully offered.

"I'm not . . . no. She didn't like what she heard, though." His voice hardened. "Never once since she came back from the movies has she been to the Mesa. Never once. She turned them down, you see. An old man died, and they wanted her to be in his place, and she turned them down. She had a husband, she said, and she had a way of her own. She would not go, and they never talked to her again."

"They don't have to," Mulder said, moving closer to the horse, keeping his voice low. "She hears them on the wind."

Quintodo stared at him, searching for mocking, for sarcasm, and his eyes narrowed when he didn't find it.

"These dead, Mr. Mulder, they didn't start until the ceremonial started."

Scully sidestepped nervously when the chestnut tried to nuzzle her again, upper lip momentarily curled to expose its teeth. "What are you saying, Mr. Quintodo? That these priests killed those people out there? And the cattle? For a . . . for some kind of—"

"No." He kept his gaze on Mulder. "Six days and six nights they stay in the kiva. Praying with the man who is to join them. Taking visions from the spirits to be sure they have made the right choice, and to show them the way until the next time. When they do all this, soon the wind blows." He made a rapid spinning motion with his free hand. "Whirlwind, Mr. Mulder. You know what I mean?"

Mulder didn't, and the man spat dryly in disgust at himself.

"Sangre Viento, Mr. Mulder. There are some who say they make the Sangre Viento."

A knock on the front door sounded thunderbolt-loud. Donna sat at her desk, a small secretary in the living room, working on the accounts. They added up, but not fast enough. If she was going to leave soon, on her terms, there would have to be more.

She was tempted to ignore whoever it was, pretend she wasn't home, then realized with a roll of her eyes that she could be seen through the room's picture window. With a martyred sigh, she scooped the ledger and papers into a drawer, pushed at her hair, and opened the door.

She couldn't believe it. "What are you doing here? It's practically the middle of the day."

"No. That's the wrong question. The right question is: have you been cheating me?"

A hand shoved her shoulder, hard, forcing her backward.

"Here's another one, *chica:* what do you think they would do if they found out?"

Mulder kept to himself on the way back to the Inn. They had declined Annie's invitation to lunch, promised to return for a nonofficial visit, and had visited the site where the couple had been murdered. It hadn't taken long; there wasn't much left to see, and when Sparrow asked, he only said it was too soon to make any kind of determination.

Once out of the car, Garson promising to see if he could set up an appointment with the hard-to-reach medical examiner, he went straight to the front desk and arranged for a rental car to be delivered that afternoon.

"I don't like being chauffeured around," he explained to Scully, leading her into the restaurant, complaining of imminent starvation. "Especially by him. He figures, but I don't know how yet."

Scully said that was the easy part. The man was clearly fond of Annie. Just as clearly, he intended, somehow, to make sure she didn't spend the rest of her life living alone.

"He's after her money?"

"I don't know. It's been known to happen. You could see he was protective; he just wasn't loving."

They took a table in the far front corner, Scully facing the white-curtained window directly behind him. They ordered, and he watched her fuss with her silverware, fuss with her napkin before spreading it on her lap.

"What?"

She didn't hide her exasperation. "I know what you're thinking, and I'm not going to let you turn this into something it isn't."

That, he thought sourly, was the problem with working with someone who knew you that well.

Still, there was no harm trying. More than once, she had saved him from making a total fool of himself, determined to keep him at least within screaming distance of reason.

"You heard what he said."

She nodded. "And it might even be possible that that couple, the Constellas, saw something they weren't supposed to. It might even be possible they were killed for it. They wouldn't be the first to die because they'd witnessed a religious event meant to be secret." She held up a knife like a finger. "Possible, I said, Mulder. Possible."

"Okay. Possible." And she smiled.

"Likely?"

He smiled back. "Don't push it. I'm still working on possible."

She started to speak, changed her mind, then changed her mind again. "But what about Paulie Deven? Don't you think it's stretching things a little to assume he saw something, too? Which he would have had to do, if you're going to keep him with the Constellas."

"Which means?"

"Mulder, it means there's no connection between the victims and the ceremony. A horrible coincidence, nothing more."

"And the . . ." He stumbled several times, making her smile, before he managed, "Sangre Viento?"

He winced when he heard himself; his Spanish was still lousy.

The waiter brought their meal, and he stared at the strips of meat, the vegetables, the salsa in the side dish, practically feeling the heat of the spices without even getting close. He knew he would regret this later, and after his first taste, knew he would have to stock up on a supply of heavy-duty antacids if he wanted to get any sleep. The trouble was, it was so good, there was no way he wouldn't eat it.

Scully, on the other hand, popped a small jalapeño into her mouth, plucked the stem from between her teeth, and said, "Not bad, not bad."

The Sangre Viento aside for the moment, he was pleased to hear that her reaction to Sparrow was the same as his. Yet neither could think of a good reason for the act, nor could they believe the man actually thought he was fooling anyone with it. It was too broad, too born of bad movies and worse television. That led them to wondering, his feelings for Annie aside, if he was somehow involved, or just a lousy cop trying to cover his ass, make them feel sorry for him so whoever he had to answer to wouldn't take his badge.

"A little farfetched," she judged when the table had been cleared and coffee served. "Not that we haven't seen it before."

"This isn't it. I don't know what it is, but this isn't it."

"Neither is that blood wind thing."

He opened his mouth, closed it, picked up a spoon and tapped it lightly against his thigh. "How can you be so sure?" He propped his elbows on the arms of his chair and clasped his hands in front of his mouth. "There are any number of recorded so-called unusual phenomena associated with meetings, especially religious, where the emotional intensity and concentration are abnormally high."

"All of them recorded by the people who were there, not by outside observers."

"They, these priests, were in a kiva. An underground chamber whose only exit and entrance, and source of air, is a single hole in the roof. There may have been herbal drugs, peyote maybe, something like that. Six days and six nights, Scully, and they all focus on a single thing—the man they're investing with their knowledge. Their history. With their power over the people they have to live with." He rocked forward, hands dropping to the table. "Can you imagine what it must be like? Day in and day out? All that energy building up there?"

Scully didn't answer him for a long time. She sipped her coffee, stared out the window, glanced around the otherwise empty room. She was about to reply when a woman appeared in the archway entrance. Short, stocky, in a severe summer-weight suit; her graying black hair pulled back into a bun. Her left hand held a purse tight to her side.

Mulder watched her hesitate, then march across the room toward them, no nonsense, all business. When she reached the table, she nodded a greeting.

"You are the agents from Washington?"

"Yes," Mulder answered. "And you are . . . ?"

"Dr. Rios. Helen Rios. I performed the autopsies on those poor people."

He stood immediately and offered her a chair while introducing her to Scully. When they were all seated again, he told her he was pleased to see her. Garson wouldn't have to make the appointment after all.

"He wouldn't have made it," the woman said.

"I . . . what?"

"You read my report?" she asked Scully.

"I did. To be honest, there weren't a lot of—"

"It's wrong."

Scully looked at the table, then back to Dr. Rios. "Excuse me?"

The woman opened her purse and pulled out a folded sheet of paper. "This is what I wrote first. What you read before is what I was told to write."

Mulder couldn't believe it.

Nor could he believe it when Scully opened the paper, skimmed it, and said, "Oh my God."

TWELVE

 After signing for the meal, Mulder moved them immediately to his room, a precaution against eyes and ears he couldn't control.

The women sat at a small round table set by the window, covered now by dark green drapes. Mulder sat on the edge of the king-size bed.

There were four lights in the room; every one of them was on.

Dr. Rios wasted no words, or time.

"New Mexico," she said, "has been trying to upgrade its image for years; decades. People still ask if you need a passport to come here. Easterners still look for cowboys and Indians battling it out in the foothills. What the politicians and businessmen do not want most of all are the hints, the stories, the urban legend–style fables that mark the state as a place where UFOs and weird cults are not only welcome, they're encouraged. Leave that kind of nonsense," Rios said, "to Arizona, and good riddance."

Then a case like this falls into their laps.

She tapped the paper she'd taken back from Scully. "Agent Mulder, it's bad enough that these poor people died the way they did. I could tell right away how it really happened, any first-year intern could have figured it out. But for the sake of appearances, because my superiors knew it was bound to hit the papers, I was asked to file a second report. The one the public would know."

It was cool in the room, but she took a handkerchief from her purse and dabbed at her forehead.

Mulder understood the chance she had taken, and the pressure she felt. He, of all people, was no stranger to either.

"I did. For the basest of reasons—I want to keep my job." She smiled grimly across the table at Scully. "I am a woman, a Hispanic woman, in a state where the Anglos and outsiders call the tunes. I am not proud of what I've done, but I make no apologies for it."

Scully kept her expression neutral, and the doctor wiped her brow again. "The official version, Agent Mulder, is that those people were flayed. They weren't."

Mulder lifted an eyebrow. "Skinned?"

"Scoured."

He choked back a laugh of disbelief. "I'm sorry, but I don't understand."

The woman checked her watch. "I have no time. Particles of dirt, pebbles, other debris were found deeply embedded not only in the muscle tissue, but also in their mouths and the back of their throats. Other indications, such as circular striation of the exposed muscles and bone and the cauterization of most of the blood vessels, point to only one conclusion."

"Scoured."

She nodded, and stood. "Like being held up against a high-speed spinning drum covered with coarse sandpaper, Agent Mulder. Or inside a cylinder lined with the same. The only thing I can't explain is the dirt." Another grim smile, another glance at her watch. "Thank you for listening. Please don't tell anyone I have seen you. If you come to my office, if Agent Garson insists we meet, all you will hear is what you've already read in the official report." She tucked the purse under her arm. "By the way, Agent Garson knows the truth, too."

Mulder rose as she left without looking back, and stayed on his feet.

A high-speed drum covered with coarse sandpaper.

"Scully—"

"Don't say it."

"But you saw—"

"I saw the pictures, yes. I read the report, yes. But given the time frame we're working with, unless Paulie's father and sister are incredibly off-base with their sense of timing, there's no way it could happen like that."

He looked down at her, pale under the table light. "It happened, Scully. It happened."

She leaned toward him, arms resting on the table. "Then explain it to me. Explain how someone could assemble an apparatus of that size, bring it down to the river without being seen, put the boy in it, kill him, take him out, and get away. Again, without anybody seeing a thing."

"The girl—"

"Saw nothing we can substantiate. Ghosts, Mulder. She said she saw ghosts."

"And whispers," he reminded her. "She also said she heard whispers."

Scully slumped back and shook her head. "What does it mean? I don't get it."

"I don't either." He yanked open the drapes, turned off the lights, and dropped into the chair opposite her. "But so far, everyone who's talked to us has—" He stopped, closed his eyes briefly, then moved to the bed and stared for a moment at the telephone on the night table.

"Mulder?"

"Konochine," he said, and picked up the

receiver. "Why do we keep bumping into the Konochine?"

"While you're at it," she said. "Give Garson a call and find out why he's so reluctant to tell us the truth."

Donna looked helplessly at the two dozen cartons stacked in her spare room. They were all ready for shipping, or for hand delivery to area shops. A permanent cold seemed to have attached itself to her spine, to her stomach. She couldn't stop shaking. She had denied cheating anyone, of course, and had even shown him the ledger to prove it. But it had been close. There had been no apology, only a lingering warning look before he left, slamming the door as he went.

She had to get out.

All the potential money in this room wasn't going to do her any good if she wasn't around to spend it.

She looked at her watch. If she hurried, she could clean out the bank account, be packed, and be out of this godforsaken state before midnight. Leave everything behind. It didn't matter. The house, her clothes . . . none of it mattered. Just take the money and get out.

But first she would have to make a phone call. She couldn't leave without saying goodbye.

* * *

Garson wasn't in his office, and no one there knew where he could be found. The secretary thought he might be at the ME's office.

The second call was to information.

When the third was finished, Mulder replaced the receiver and began to wonder.

"What?" Scully asked.

"According to his sister, Paulie picked up a piece of jewelry from one of the local shops. A silver pendant of some kind." Mulder looked up. "She thinks it was Konochine."

"And?"

"And I don't remember seeing it as being with his effects."

"Such as they were," she reminded him.

"Whatever. It wasn't there." He rose, and paced until Scully's warning groan put him back in his chair. "That woman, the one who handles the crafts."

She flipped open a notebook, paged through it, and said, "Falkner."

"You want to take a ride?"

"Mulder—"

"The connection, Scully. You can't deny we have a connection."

The rental car had been delivered, and the clerk at the front desk gave him a map and directions to the address he had found in the telephone book. The parking lot was on the north side of the Inn, through a gated entry in the side wall. As he slipped behind the wheel, Mulder noted that the car seemed to have every gadget known to Detroit, except perhaps an orbital trajectory tracking system.

It took him a few seconds to get oriented, and a few seconds more before he convinced himself that he wasn't charging headlong into foolishness. The how of the murders was still beyond him, in spite of Dr. Rios's description. Concentrate on the who and the why, however, and the how would come wagging its tail behind them.

He hoped.

As he pulled out onto the street and headed north, Scully inhaled quickly.

"What?"

They passed a series of four small stores in a common one-story building. A man stood in front of one of them, not bothering to conceal his interest in the car.

"Last night," she said. "I didn't see him clearly, but there was a man at the gate, watching me."

He checked the rearview mirror.

The man, face hidden by the bill of his cap, still watched.

There was no flip of a mental coin. Mulder swung the wheel around, made a U-turn, made another to pull alongside the stores.

The man hadn't moved.

Scully lowered her window. "Do you want something?" she asked calmly.

Leon Ciola swaggered over and leaned down. "You the feds?"

With one hand still on the wheel, Mulder leaned over, curious about the fine scars that swept across the man's face. "Special Agent Mulder, Special Agent Scully. Who are you?"

"Leon Ciola."

"You've been watching us. Why?"

Ciola spread his arms wide in a mocking bow, smiling impudently. "Always like to know who's in town, *amigos*, that's all. It's very dull around here, you know? Not much to do. The sun's too hot. Not much work for a man like me."

"What is a man like you?" Scully said.

"Ex-con. They didn't tell you that?"

No, Mulder thought; there's a lot they haven't told us.

Then he spotted a faint racial resemblance to Nando Quintodo. "You're from the Mesa?"

Ciola's smile didn't falter. "Very good, *amigo*. Most people think I look Apache." Fingers fluttered across his face. "The scars. They make me look mean."

"Are you?"

The smile vanished. "I'm a son of a bitch, Agent Mulder. A good thing to know."

He's not bragging, Mulder thought; he's not warning, either.

Ciola glanced up and down the street, then placed a hand on the window well. "Sheriff Sparrow will tell you that I have killed a man. It's true. Maybe more, who knows? He'll tell you, when he gets around to it, that I probably killed those stupid tourists. I didn't, Agent Mulder. I have more important things to do."

He tipped his cap to Scully and backed away, interview over.

Mulder nodded to him, straightened, and pulled slowly away from the curb. The man chilled him. What chilled him more, however, was the fact that Sparrow hadn't said a word about him. An obvious suspect, a self-confessed killer ex-con, and the sheriff had, conveniently or otherwise, kept Ciola's name to himself.

"Scully, do you get the feeling we've dropped down the rabbit hole?"

She didn't answer.

A glance at her profile showed him lips so taut they were bloodless.

He didn't question her. Something about the man, something he hadn't caught, struck a nerve. Sooner or later, she would tell him what it was. As it was, he had to deal with street signs he could barely read because they were too small, and the vehicles impatiently lining up behind him because he was driving slow enough to try to read the damn signs.

The sun didn't help.

It flared off everything, and bleached that which wasn't already bleached.

Everywhere there were signs of a town struggling to find the right way to grow—obviously new shops, shops that had gone out of business, houses and buildings in varying stages of construction or repair. It was either very exciting to live here now, or very frightening.

"There," Scully said.

He turned left, toward the river, and found himself on a street where lots were large and vacant, spotted only once in a while by small, one-story houses in either brick or fake adobe. A drab place, made more so by the gardens and large bushes flowering violent colors. No toys in the driveways. The few cars at the curbs seemed abandoned.

He parked in front of a ranch house whose front window was buried by a tangled screen of roses. A Cherokee parked in the pitted drive faced the street. As they got out, he saw a suitcase by the driver's door.

"Somebody's going on vacation."

"I don't think so," she said, nodding toward the two other suitcases sitting on the stoop. "Not unless she's planning to stay away for six months."

He knocked on the screen door.

No one answered.

He knocked again, and the inner door was

opened by a young woman with a briefcase in one hand.

"I don't want any," she said.

Scully held up her ID. "Special Agent Scully, Special Agent Mulder, FBI. Are you Donna Falkner?"

It didn't take any special instinct to realize the woman was afraid. Mulder opened the screen door carefully and said, "We'd just like to talk to you, Ms. Falkner. It won't take a minute, and then you can take your trip."

"How did you know that?" Donna demanded, her voice pitched high enough to crack. Then she followed Mulder's gesture toward the suitcases. "Oh."

"Just a few minutes," Scully assured her.

The woman's shoulders slumped. "Oh, what the hell, why not. How much worse can it get?"

THIRTEEN

X The air conditioning had been shut off. The room was stifling. The woman hasn't left yet, Mulder thought, and already the house feels deserted.

Donna grabbed a ladder-back chair from in front of a small desk and turned it around. When she sat, shoulders still slumped, she held the briefcase in her lap, looking as if she wanted to hold it against her chest. Scully took a seat on a two-cushion couch, pen and notebook in hand; Mulder remained standing, leaning a shoulder against the wall just inside the room's entry.

It kept him in partial shadow; it kept the woman in full light.

"So," she said resignedly. "What do you want to know?"

"The Konochine," Mulder told her, and saw her gaze dart in his direction.

"What about them?"

"You sell their jewelry," Scully said, shifting the woman's attention back the other way. "We were told they didn't like the outside world very much."

"Hardly at all," Donna answered. Her shoulders rose a little. "I got chased off the res once, back before I knew what I was doing." She shifted the briefcase to the floor beside her. "See, they're not the only Indians I deal with, but they give me the most trouble. Or did, anyway. There's this man—"

"Nick Lanaya?" Mulder said.

"Yeah. He's one of the out-and-backers. You know, got out, came back? Well, we met at a party once, got to talking—he's very easy to talk to, kind of like a priest, if you know what I mean. Anyway, he knew his people needed money, and after he asked around, he knew I'd be able to get them a fair price for the work."

Scully moved a hand to draw her attention again. "How mad are the ones who don't want outside contact?"

Donna frowned, the understanding of what

Scully meant slow in arriving. "Oh. Oh! Hey, not that mad. God, no. You think they killed those poor people?" She dismissed the notion with a wave. "Jesus, no. They talk a lot, yell a lot, but Nick just yells right back. He's—" She stopped, frozen, as though something had just occurred to her. "Tell you, though, the guy you should be talking to is Leon Ciola."

"We've met," Mulder said dryly.

"You're kidding." Her right hand drifted down to brush at the case. "You know he was in the state pen, up by Santa Fe? Killed a man in a bar fight." Her left hand draw a line across her throat. Slowly. "Nearly cut his head off. I don't know how he got out. A good lawyer, I guess."

"Where are you going?" Scully asked.

"Vacation," Donna replied instantly.

"You take more clothes than Scully," Mulder said with a laugh.

"I'll be away for a while."

"Who takes care of the business? Nick?"

She shrugged. "Mostly, yeah."

Scully closed her notebook. "You have no control over what you receive from the Mesa? Or who buys them retail?"

"Nope. Nick chooses the pieces, I choose the shops. After that, it's the guy who has the most money."

Mulder pushed away from the wall. "What if

somebody who didn't know any better just drove onto the reservation?"

"Nothing." Donna retrieved her case. "No one would talk to them, probably. Sooner or later, they'd get the hint and leave."

"And if they didn't?"

"You mean like me?" She laughed; it was false. "I'm pushy, Agent Mulder. I pushed too far. Chasing is all that would happen, believe me." She stood and looked none too subtly at the door. "I still say you should check Ciola. He has a knife and . . ." She shuddered for effect.

Scully rose as well. "Thank you, Ms. Falkner. We appreciate the time."

"No problem." She led them to the stoop. "If you don't mind, though, I have a plane to catch, okay?"

Mulder thanked her again, asked her to call Agent Garson if there was anything else she thought of before she left, and got behind the wheel, cursing himself soundly for forgetting to leave the windows down.

The sun out there, and an oven in here. He set the air conditioning to high and hurry up about it and drove off, taking his time, while Scully watched Donna Falkner in the outside mirror. When they turned the corner, Scully said, "She relaxed very quickly."

"Yeah. Because we didn't ask her about what she thought we would."

"Which was?"

"Scully, if I knew that, I would have asked her."

She grunted disbelief; he knew what she was thinking. There were times when asking questions got you answers, but not necessarily when you wanted them. There were times when it was better to spin a web and see who tried to break free.

Donna was breaking free.

Once she got on that plane, New Mexico would never see her again.

Scully looked over. "How are you going to stop her?"

He gestured toward the backseat, asking her to grab his denim jacket. When she did, his portable phone fell out of the inside pocket.

"Garson?" she said.

"Material witness to an active investigation."

"But she isn't, Mulder."

"No, maybe not. But he can delay her long enough to miss her flight. Maybe discourage her enough to wait until tomorrow."

She called, discovered Garson couldn't be reached, and demanded to speak to an agent on duty. After convincing him they weren't kidding about Falkner, she asked where the Constella van was being held.

"Right here," she said when she hung up. "A lot behind a sheriff's substation."

"Why do you want to see it?"

"You wanted to see Ann Hatch, and look what it got us. I want to see that van."

"And what do you mean, I take too many clothes when I go on a trip?"

The substation was little more than a double-wide on cinder blocks, only a sign on the door announcing its function. The parking area in front was only big enough for four vehicles, and the tree that cast a weak shade over the building looked about ready to collapse at any second. Beyond the tree was another lot, fenced in with chain-link and topped with concertina wire. Within were a handful of cars, a pickup, and a van.

Sheriff Sparrow was outside waiting when Mulder pulled in off the street.

"Garson works fast," Scully said when they stopped.

"Your tax dollars at work."

Sparrow waved them over to a padlocked gate in the fence. "Looking for anything in particular?" he asked as the gate swung free and they walked in.

"You never know," Mulder told him.

The van was at the back, dusty enough to ward off the sun. Mulder shaded his eyes and looked through the side and front windows, then asked Sparrow for the key.

"What for?"

"To get inside." He rapped a knuckle against the sliding side door. "You never know."

Sparrow grumbled, complained that he'd left the keys inside, and headed back to the trailer.

"Mulder?"

She was on the passenger side, and he took his time joining her. The heat was brutal, worse than the day before, and he understood now why life was so deliberate in this part of the world. Anything faster than a crawl on a day like today meant sure heatstroke, and a tub packed in ice.

"So?"

She pointed to the side.

He looked and saw the dust; then he saw what lay under the dust.

He used a palm to wipe the metal clean, and yelped when the heat scorched him. "Damn!" He shook his hand, blew on it, and pulled a handkerchief from his pocket.

"Be careful," she said. "It's hot." When he gave her a look, she only shrugged and added, "Your tax dollars at work."

There were two large tinted windows, one in the sliding door, the other at the back. He shook the handkerchief out, then folded it in quarters to form a makeshift dusting pad. Hunkering down, balancing on his toes, he swiped at the dust and dirt first, to knock off what he could before he started rubbing.

"What the hell you looking for?" Sparrow said, tossing the keys to Scully.

"This was a rental," Mulder said without looking up.

"Yep. So?"

"New, then, right?"

"Probably." The sheriff leaned over him, squinting at the panel. "So?"

"So I guess Mr. Constella wasn't much of a driver."

He didn't have to rub. When the area was clear, he rose and took a step back, waiting for Sparrow to comment. He was also waiting to hear why the man hadn't noticed it days ago. Or, if he had, why he hadn't said anything.

From the window to the bottom of the frame, the paint had been scraped off, right down to bare metal. The dust had been thick, the van having sat here for more than a week in the sheriff's custody. A glint of that bare metal was what had caught Scully's attention.

"Well, I'll be damned." Sparrow hitched his belt. "Run up against a stone wall, boulder, something like that, looks like."

"I don't think so." Mulder ran a finger lightly over the surface. "No appreciable indentation, so there was no real collision."

Scully stepped in front of them and peered at it closely, shifted and sighted along the side to the rear bumper. "If there was, it wouldn't be in just this one place." When she straightened, she leaned close to the window. Touched it with a forefinger. Took the handkerchief and wiped the glass clean. "Scrapes here, too."

"Road dirt," Sparrow said. "You get it all the time out here, dust and all, going the speeds you do."

She ignored him for the moment, using the finger to trace the damage's outline, right to the strip above the window. "Whatever it was, it was big. Man-high, at least."

"Like I said, a boulder."

"Come on, Sheriff," Mulder said, having had enough of his forced ignorance. "Scully's right. A collision would have produced damage wider than this, and by the force of it, at the least this window would have been cracked, if not smashed."

He scratched under his jaw, and leaned close again.

"Agent Mulder, this is—"

"Do you have a magnifying glass?"

He heard the man snort his disgust, but the expected argument didn't happen. Sparrow trudged away, muttering about how the damn feds think they know everything, just loudly enough.

Scully unlocked the passenger door and stood

back to let the heat out. Then she climbed in and through the two front seats to the back. Mulder couldn't see her until she rapped on the window and beckoned.

He knelt on the passenger seat and leaned over the top. The two rows of bench seats had been taken out, leaving the holding rails behind. The floor and walls were covered with alternating swatches of vivid purple and dull brown carpeting.

"This is a love nest?" he said, wincing at the garish combination.

"Love is blind, Mulder." She was on her knees, poking at a loose section of carpet with her pen.

"In here it would have to be."

"Got it."

She rocked back on her heels and held up the pen. Dangling from it was a length of silver chain. She followed when Mulder backed out, and dropped the chain into his palm. "That's not a store chain. It's handmade." She prodded it with the pen, shifting it as he watched. "I'll bet it's not silver-plated, either."

He brought the palm closer to his eyes.

The links were longer than he would have expected, and not as delicately thin as they first appeared. Neither were they the same length.

She took the chain back, grasping each end between thumb and forefinger. Tugged once.

"Strong. You couldn't yank this off someone's neck without sawing halfway through it."

"Konochine."

She gave him a *maybe* tilt of her head, and headed back to the car to fetch a plastic evidence bag from her purse.

"Bring a couple," he called after her, and glanced at his watch.

Sparrow still hadn't returned; Mulder finally lost the rest of his patience. He marched over to the trailer, yanked open the door, and stepped in. The sheriff was seated behind one of three desks in the room, his feet up, his hat off, a flask at his lips.

He looked startled when he saw Mulder, but he didn't move until he had finished his drink. "It's hot out there," he said.

"It's going to get hotter," Mulder told him, not bothering to suppress his anger. "Give me the glass, then get one of your people ready to take some evidence to Garson's technicians. I'll call him myself to tell him what to look for."

Sparrow glared as he set the flask onto the desk. "I don't believe I heard the magic word, Agent Mulder."

Mulder just looked at him, and "FBI" was all he said.

FOURTEEN

X He couldn't see Scully when he returned to the lot, slapping the magnifying glass hard against his leg. He was angry and disappointed, not nearly as much at the sheriff as at himself. Losing control like that, pulling rank, wasn't his style. Working with local law was something he had learned to do years ago, knowing that their assistance was just as vital to investigations as his own federal agents. What he had just done was a violation not only of policy, but his own code.

"Scully?"

It was dumb.

"Hey, Scully!"

It was stupid.

"Over here, Mulder."

But boy, did it feel good.

He found her standing next to what used to be a sleek Jaguar. Now most of its windows were shattered, the windshield web-cracked, the racing-green paint pocked and scored from front to back, and the roof crushed as though someone had dropped a flatcar on it.

"Our drunk driver?" he asked.

"I don't know. I think so. Look at this."

He went around to the side, and saw the same pattern of scouring she had uncovered on the van, only this time it was wider.

"Invisible car," he said.

She lifted a questioning hand. "I give up, Mulder. What's going on?" A closer look at his face. "Never mind. I think I'd rather know what happened in there."

There was no chance to answer. The trailer door slammed gunshot loud, and Sparrow stomped toward them. The way his hand chopped the air, Mulder figured he was having one hell of an argument with himself. By the time he reached them, the argument was over.

He stood with one hand resting on the handle of his holstered gun, while the other folded a stick of gum into his mouth. Then he pulled off his sunglasses by pinching them at the bridge and sliding.

"I'll take the evidence in myself." It wasn't an order, it wasn't a demand. It was an offer of truce.

"That's fine with me, sir," Mulder said, accepting the offer.

"Chuck." The sheriff chewed rapidly.

Mulder grinned. "I don't think so."

"Me neither. My mother hated it. She always said it wasn't the name of anything but chopped meat." He pushed the sunglasses back on. "So, FBI, what's so important you got to rush it into the city?"

While Scully explained about the partial necklace chain, Mulder went back to the van and, with the magnifying glass and the tip of a blade on his Swiss army knife, pried loose samples of debris caught in the deep gouges on the door. He did the same to the car, sealed his findings in the bags, and handed them over.

Uneasy, but more at ease, they walked back to the office, grateful for the cool respite. Scully tagged and numbered the bags. Mulder called Garson's office, told them what to expect and what he wanted done.

"That shouldn't take very long," the secretary said confidently.

"Have you found Agent Garson yet?"

"No sir, I sure haven't."

He gave her his number and instructed her to have Garson call as soon as he came in. When he

asked whether Donna Falkner had been inter-
cepted, he was told that she had been, by one of
the other agents. Apparently she hadn't been very
happy, certainly not when she was brought back
to the Silver Avenue office, where she currently
was giving a statement.

"A statement? About what?"

"I wouldn't know, sir. I'm only the secretary.
They only tell me what I need to know."

Sure, he thought; and all the rest is magic.

He perched on the edge of the nearest empty
desk and wiped his brow with a sleeve.

Sparrow was back in his chair. "You reckon it's
the Konochine somehow? I figured that, what
with you talking to Donna and all."

"I don't see how it can't be, now. There are too
many connections."

"A lead, anyway," Scully added.

"Oh boy." The sheriff reached for his flask,
changed his mind, and propped his feet up
instead. "Trouble is, there's a couple hundred of
them. It can't be all—" Suddenly he snapped
upright, boots stamping the floor. "Son of a
bitch!"

Mulder looked first to Scully before saying,
"Leon Ciola."

The sheriff's jaw sagged. "Damn, Mulder,
you're good." He drummed his fingers against
his cheek thoughtfully, then reached for his
phone. "There's somebody you should meet.

He'll be able to tell you what you want know about who you need to know about. Lanaya. I already told you about him. Believe it or not, he still lives on the res."

"What about Ciola?"

Sparrow held up a finger as the connection was made, winced as he made arrangements with the dealer to meet at the Inn after dinner that evening, winced again and rubbed his ear as he hung up. "Storm coming," he explained. "Static'll deafen you sometimes."

Thank God, Mulder thought; at least it'll get cooler.

"Ciola," he reminded Sparrow.

"Bastard. Pure and simple bastard. Got sent up for murder, got a lawyer who found a hole and squeezed the son of a bitch through it. There's not much I can do but keep an eye out, and hope he doesn't lose his temper again."

It didn't take special intuition to figure out the man not only hated Ciola, he was afraid of him.

"You thinking he's involved with this?"

"You have to admit, he's a likely candidate."

"Nope, don't think so."

Mulder was surprised, and let the sheriff know it.

"Not his style," Sparrow explained. "He's all intimidation and reputation. The man he killed, it was over quick and dirty. These people . . . that took patience."

"But not much time, Sheriff," Scully said. "The Deven boy, remember?"

He granted her that reluctantly, but insisted it couldn't have been Ciola. "There's a reason for those people, Agent Scully. We just ain't found it yet. With Leon, there doesn't have to be one."

"Heat of the moment," Mulder suggested.

"Got it in one."

Scully seemed doubtful, but didn't argue.

The sheriff accepted her silence without comment, looked around the station, then carefully locked the plastic bags into an attache case he pulled from a bottom drawer. "Better get going. I want to get back before the storm." He walked to the back and radioed one of his men, telling him where he'd be and for how long; he called a central dispatcher with the same information, for intercepting any calls; he spat his gum into a wastebasket, opened a wardrobe on the far wall, and took down a clean, blocked hat.

When he saw Mulder staring, he pointed to the hat on the desk. "That's my comfort hat, had it for years." He flicked the brim on the one he had on. "This is my showing-up-in-the-city hat. Pretty dumb, ain't it."

Scully laughed, and Mulder could only nod as Sparrow walked with them to their car.

"Check it out, folks," he said, pointing over the trailer. "Be inside when it happens."

Mulder looked, and couldn't believe that clouds that massive, and that high, could assemble so quickly. Shaped like anvils, boiling at the edges, they had already buried most of the western blue.

"My God, Scully, we're going to drown."

He drove back to the motel as fast as he dared, which still wasn't fast enough for the others on the road. They passed him on the left, on the right, and would have driven over him if the car had been low enough.

"Calm down," Scully said when the engine died. "We've still got some work to do while we wait for Lanaya."

The bone pile stirred as the wind brushed over it, dust in tan clouds passing through ribs and eye sockets, through a gaping hole in one of the skulls.

A scorpion scuttled across the curled horn of a ram.

In the center, using the pelvic bone of a stallion for a temporary stool, a man stirred the loose earth with the point of a knife. Designs were fashioned, and erased; words were written, and vanished. He glanced up only once, to check the storm's approach, returning to his work only when he saw the lightning, and didn't hear the thunder.

It would move fast.

He would move faster.

Donna Falkner slammed into her house, slammed the door shut behind her, flung a suitcase across the living room, and began to scream her outrage. She kicked at the nearest wall, picked up the desk chair and hurled it down the hall; she grabbed the couch cushions and tried to rip them open with her nails, tossed them aside, and dropped to the floor, sobbing.

It wasn't fair.

It wasn't goddamn fair.

All she had to do was get on the goddamn plane, and she was out of here. Gone. Lost in another city, where they never heard of Indians except on TV, never bothered with Southwest crafts except in fancy boutiques that overpriced everything from a wallet to a brooch. Gone. New name, new hair, new everything.

Gone.

Now the FBI wanted her, and *he* wanted her, and there was nothing she could do about it but sit around and wait.

She punched the floor.

She screamed again, cheeks florid, teeth bared.

The sunlight began to dim, and the thorns of the rosebushes began to scratch lightly against the windows.

Suddenly she couldn't breathe, made a double fist with her hands, and pressed it against her chest. Harder. Gulping for air. Rocking on her buttocks until she thought she would faint. Tears streaming down her cheeks, dripping off her chin, coating her lips with the taste of salt.

When the attack passed, she let herself fall backward slowly, seeing nothing but tiny cracks in the plaster ceiling, forming them into images that made her weep again.

The telephone rang.

She wiped her eyes with the backs of her hands and sat up. She had no intention of answering it. Let it ring. If it was those agents who had come to see her, they could just come over on their own. The hell with them. The hell with them all.

When she stood, she swayed; when she walked down the short hall toward the bathroom, she staggered. When she reached the bathroom, she looked at her reflection, gagged . . . and giggled. Touched the tip of her reflection's nose with a finger and told it there was nothing to worry about, nothing she couldn't handle.

What she would do was, if they wouldn't let her fly, then fuck it, she would drive. By the time they realized she was gone, she would be . . . gone.

She giggled again.

Gone, but not forgotten.

Gone, and goddamn rich.

Wash up, she ordered; wash up, change your clothes, get the damn money, and be . . . gone.

What the hell are you so worried about?

She didn't know.

Suddenly, she didn't know.

She hurried into the spare room, squinted through the small window, and figured by the sky she had maybe an hour before the storm arrived. If it arrived. They had a bad habit of being all show and no action sometimes. Not that it mattered. Only a fool would tempt clouds like that on an open road.

Another giggle.

Screw 'em.

Now that she wasn't flying, she could load the Cherokee to the gills, take a little inventory to pad the mattress. The not-so-perfect plan, but better than nothing. Nothing would mean sitting around, waiting for things to happen.

She grabbed a carton and headed for the door.

Sand stirred, lifting sluggishly from the ground as if drawn by a weak magnet.

Nearby, a dead leaf quivered.

A twig shifted, rolled an inch, and stopped.

The sand settled a few seconds later.

Nothing moved.

FIFTEEN

The shower was wonderful.

After crawling around the van and automobile in the sun all that time, Scully was drenched with sweat, caked and streaked with dust, and ready to scream. In spite of the silver chain, in spite of what Mulder had dug from the vehicles' sides, they hadn't accomplished very much.

What frustrated her was a combination of the case itself, which seemed to be going nowhere fast, and the certain knowledge that she had already seen the break point and had missed it. Something small. Something so obvious she had overlooked it. The purloined letter in New Mexico.

The storm didn't help.

The clouds, frightening black and impossibly huge, were still out there, still in the middle distance. If they moved, she couldn't tell. They sat there, not small enough to be lurking, and too large to even be called looming. There was nothing ahead of them but a steady, hot wind.

They were also tired. The mix of altitude and heat had sapped them without their realizing it. When they reached the motel, it was a mutual decision to clean up and rest for an hour, then meet again to see what they could come up with before their meeting with Nick Lanaya.

So she used the shower to make her comfortable again, to drain the afternoon's tension from her shoulders and limbs, and to let her mind roam, seeking pathways and the places where they might possibly join into something concrete she could follow, something hopeful.

When it didn't happen immediately, she was mildly annoyed, but she didn't mind. It would come eventually; of that she was confident.

She took her time dressing, sat on the edge of her bed, and gazed at the window, scowling at the tension she could feel building again. She rolled her shoulders, massaged them one at a time, to get rid of it; it didn't work. She stretched until her joints threatened to pop or separate, deliberately groaning aloud; it didn't work.

Maybe it was just anticipation of the storm.

The clouds must have moved closer while she had been in the bathroom. The sunlight held considerably less glare, a hint of false twilight filtering into the front courtyard. By that part of the bench tree she could see, the wind had died down as well.

It seemed that the outside had decided to do nothing but wait until the storm made up its mind whether to strike or not.

"Damn," she whispered.

No wonder she was still tense. That was exactly what she was doing. Waiting, not acting. Some son of a bitch had butchered three innocent people, and all she could do was sit here like a lump and wait for the damn rain.

She snapped to her feet, grabbed her shoulder bag, decided the hell with the hat, and hurried outside.

No one in the courtyard and, when she couldn't help looking, no one standing at the gate.

The image of Ciola's face so close to her own made her pause and shudder. Those scars, and those dead eyes . . . she shuddered again and knocked hard on Mulder's door, one heel tapping impatiently. When he answered, naked to the waist and drying his hair with a towel, she said, "Get decent, Mulder. We're going out again."

* * *

The sand stirred.

The leaf quivered.

"You're the one who made the connections," Scully said as he pulled on a shirt. "So why wait?"

"Scully, we haven't been here twenty-four hours."

"That doesn't answer my question: Why wait?"

He couldn't think of a good answer, and didn't especially want to, not when she practically sparked with energy like this. It was best, always best, to go along for the ride. Besides, she was right. With too many signs pointing to the Konochine, it only made sense to pay an official visit to the reservation. The only problem was, he thought they ought to have a guide, someone who knew who they should talk to, preferably someone who knew the language.

"The sheriff."

"He's in Albuquerque, remember?"

"Falkner."

"They rode her out on a rail."

She tapped a fingernail on the table. "Lanaya would be perfect, but we don't know how to get in touch with him."

They tried the phone book, but no luck; they tried the sheriff's dispatcher, and had the same result. A call to Falkner brought no answer; Scully let the phone ring twenty times before hanging up in disgust.

Neither one of them even breathed Leon Ciola's name.

He switched on a lamp without thinking. "We could always go out to the ranch," he suggested, not really too happy with the idea.

Neither was Scully, from her reaction. At the moment, however, there was no place else to turn. And, he added, reaching for his gun and holster to clip on his belt, it didn't especially have to be Annie. In fact, it probably shouldn't be, if what the foreman had told them was true. Quintodo himself would do just as well, assuming he was willing. It wasn't a raid; they were simply looking for information.

Which, he thought glumly, they probably wouldn't get anyway. If the Indians wanted as little to do as possible with whites in general, representatives of the government in Washington, especially the law, would no doubt be treated as if they had the plague.

Then he opened the door, took a quick step back, and said, "You have an ark handy?"

The storm had finally reached them.

Scully made a wordless sound of amazement as they watched the rain pound the courtyard in dark and light streaks shot through with silver, pockets of steam rising from the ground in swirling patches that were shredded and whisked away. It was so heavy, they could barely see the wall.

Scully turned on the rest of the lights and rubbed her upper arms. "Close the door, it's cold."

Mulder didn't mind. After walking around in a furnace all day, the sensation was luxurious.

And the rain fascinated him.

"It can't last long," she said, although it sounded like a question.

He had seen downpours before, but this was more than that, this was an outright deluge; it didn't seem possible it could last for more than a few minutes. There couldn't be that much water in the sky.

Ten minutes later he closed the door and shrugged. "I guess we're stuck. Unless you want to try it anyway."

"Out there? In that?"

Looking out the window didn't do any good; the rain smothered it, completely obliterating the outside world.

He wished, however, that the wind would rise. It didn't seem natural, all that rain and no wind to whip it.

Scully moved over to the bed and picked up the receiver. "I'll try Garson again. I'd like to know what he's been doing all day."

He would, too. He had already run through a couple of scenarios, neither of which he liked.

He doubted seriously that the man was upset because of their arrival; they were all supposed to be working the same territory no matter what state that territory was in. He also didn't think Garson was part of what they were looking for; it felt wrong. Nothing more; it just felt wrong.

Scully hung up. "Nothing. Sparrow's been there, but there are no results yet."

Rain slapped at the door, a little wind at last.

A constant thudding overhead, like an army marching across the roof.

"Talk to me, Mulder," Scully said then.

He sat at the table, drew invisible patterns on the surface to focus him and, at the same time, to let him think aloud without built-in restrictions.

"It's a cliché," he said slowly, "but maybe it's true here, who knows? What we know for sure is that Paulie and the Constellas had Konochine jewelry. Except for that partial chain you found, it was gone when the bodies were discovered. Destroyed or taken, we don't know yet. But it's gone.

"Maybe this Lanaya brought out the wrong kind. Maybe it has some religious or traditional significance we don't understand yet. Everyone we've talked to has made a big deal of telling us they don't want contact, minimal contact at best. So it's possible that exposing those pieces to the outside could be considered a form of sacrilege.

There might be some on the reservation who would do anything to get it back."

"You're right, it is a cliché." She leaned forward and rested her forearms on her thighs. "And don't forget, Lanaya is one of their own. He wouldn't make a mistake like that. Not even a careless one."

"Then maybe it's the very fact that the pieces went out at all."

"He's been doing it for years."

"He's been fighting them for years."

"But he's still been doing it."

Right, he thought; and by now, after all this time, hundreds of people must have Konochine rings and necklaces and who knew what else? Hundreds, at least, but only three had died.

A damp chill filtered into the room.

The light flickered once and settled, startling him into the realization that there was no thunder, no lightning. How could clouds like that, with all that power, not have thunder and lightning?

Scully rose and walked to the bathroom door, walked back and sat again. "I'd still like to know how it was done."

"Scoured. Dr. Rios said scoured."

"How?"

He almost said, "Sentient Brillo," but changed his mind when he saw the *don't you dare, Mulder* look on her face.

Instead, he answered, "I haven't a clue."

"Yes!" She slapped her leg angrily. "Yes, damnit, we *do* have a clue! We just don't know what it is."

There was no response to exasperation like that, so he drew patterns again, over and over, while he listened to the thunder the army made on the roof.

"Sangre Viento," he said at last.

"It has a nice ring, but what does it mean, aside from the translation?"

Patterns; always patterns.

He watched the finger move, trying not to control it consciously. Automatic writing that did nothing but draw senseless patterns.

Thirty minutes after the storm began, he tilted his chair back, reached over and opened the door, squinting against a spray that dropped ice on his cheeks. "This is impossible. When the hell is it going to end?"

And the rain stopped.

He almost toppled backward at the abruptness of the cessation. One second he couldn't see an inch past the tree, the next all there was were glittering droplets falling from the leaves and eaves, and a slow runoff of water along narrow, shallow trenches set along the paths.

He looked at Scully and said, "Am I good, or what?"

* * *

Donna whispered a prayer when the rain finally ended and the sun came out. One more quick turn around the house and a check of the back yard, and she would leave. The Cherokee was packed; she had never unpacked. It had been a stupid idea anyway, thinking she could use the rain for cover. She wouldn't have made it half a mile on the interstate before she would have been forced to pull over. This way she was calmer, and had a clearer head.

She had had time to think.

Now it was time to fish or cut bait.

The bone pile had been touched by only a fringe of the storm, washed clean and gleaming.

The water had been taken by leaves and roots and the porous desert floor; there were no puddles, and there was no wind.

Nevertheless, the sand stirred.

SIXTEEN

X Mulder stepped outside and inhaled deeply several times. Too many scents mingled for him to identify, but they were sweet, and he was pleased. He had caught Scully's determination, and with the dust washed away, even the prospects of success seemed more bright.

You're pushing it, he told himself, and didn't much care. It felt pretty good, and he took that where he could get it.

Scully followed, checking to be sure the door locked behind her. A detour to the front desk assured them that the clerk had Mulder's portable phone number and would relay calls or messages as soon as they were received.

Just as they were about to turn away from the desk, Scully gave a nod toward the side entrance. "I think we have company."

A tall man in denim and a ponytail walked toward them, taking off his hat as he approached. "Agent Mulder? Agent Scully?"

Mulder nodded warily.

The man held out his hand. "Nick Lanaya. We were supposed to meet later." He cocked a lean hip as he shifted his weight. "Sorry I'm early, but I took a chance catching you. I was going to stop at a friend's first, but the storm . . ."

"Actually," Scully said, "your timing is perfect. We were about to drive out to the Mesa."

His eyes widened. "Alone?"

"No. We were hoping someone from the Double-H would go along. But," she added with a smile, "now you're here, which is exactly what we need."

"Damn right about that," he said, matching her with a smile of his own. "Today's Thursday. You go there today, they'll probably shoot you."

"What?" Mulder said.

"Well, not really shoot you, Agent Mulder, but you wouldn't have gotten in. It's a . . . call it a holy day. Kind of like Sunday, only a little more intense." He used the hat to gesture toward the restaurant. "So what do you say we have something to eat? Chuck said you had a few questions, and I answer better on a full stomach."

Not long after they were at a table, this time near the entrance. Other diners had already begun to arrive, and the room was more lively, more cheerful than last time. The contrast was startling, and it took Mulder a few minutes before he was able to concentrate on what Lanaya told him.

Anecdotes at first, as their meal arrived and they ate, trying to give them a feel for his people. They were conservative, hard-working, and surprisingly, they didn't feel at all oppressed.

"They've been at Sangre Viento since their Time began. No one has ever defeated them in war badly enough to drive them out, although the Apache gave them a hard time for a while, a hundred years or so back, and the white man hasn't seen any need to do anything but leave them pretty much alone." He seemed slightly embarrassed. "To tell you the truth, it makes them kind of smug."

Scully brushed the corner of her mouth with a napkin. "I understand you're an important person there."

Lanaya closed his eyes as he laughed, shook his head and waved his fork. "Lord, no. Important?" He laughed again. "Not the way you mean, no. Some sort of authority figure, a position of power, something like that?"

"Something like that, yes."

"Nope. Sorry. I'm important only in that I

keep their contacts with the outside healthy, that's all. They're not stupid, Agent Scully. They don't live primitively; not by their standards, anyway. They just pick and choose what they want from the white man's world, that's all. Some have TV, everybody has a radio. Schooling is important. I'm not the only one who went to college."

"But you went back."

"Yes. Yes, I went back. Often there are ties too strong to be broken." His left hand moved to his chest and away, but not before Mulder spotted a bulge there.

A medicine bag, he thought; he carries his power with him.

"Anyway, what is it, exactly, that you want to know?"

Mulder watched Scully's smile, and hid one of his own. The man was taken with her, and whether he knew it or not, Scully had already gotten more from him than he probably wanted them to know.

They.

He said *they* instead of *we*.

Scully's next question was predictable, and Mulder couldn't help feeling a faint disappointment at the answer.

"No, there's no significance to any of the things I bring out for Donna to sell. Traditional designs, that's all." He chuckled. "Once in a while, the designs are . . . borrowed, shall we say? The artisans get bored doing the same thing all the time."

"You mean they fake it? Pass their work off as someone else's?"

"I mean they get bored, Agent Scully. What they use, they make their own."

They again.

Mulder began to wonder.

Suddenly the man grunted and clutched at his stomach. Scully was on her feet immediately, but he waved her away. "It's okay," he said, gasping a little, his eyes watering. "Took me by surprise, is all."

Scully stood by him anyway. "What did?"

Lanaya gestured toward his plate. "Ulcer, I think."

"What? You have an ulcer and you eat this stuff?" She rolled her eyes and took her seat. "You're out of your mind."

"Maybe." He took a roll of antacid tablets from his pocket and popped one into his mouth. "No, definitely. But I keep hoping I'll get used to it before I die."

"Don't worry, you won't," she told him. "Because that stuff will end up killing you."

He laughed, and Mulder managed a polite smile in response.

He was getting damn tired of people lying to his face.

* * *

There was someone in the backyard.

She heard movement as she dropped her suitcase into the passenger seat, and swore. With hardly any neighbors to speak of, who the hell would be out there? Unless it was a stray cat, or . . . she glared. Or a goddamn coyote.

She hurried into the house, yanked open a desk drawer, and pulled out a wood-stock .38. She had never given a damn what the cautions were; it was always loaded. A single woman living alone would scarcely have the time to load if someone broke in in the middle of the night.

She hefted it, thumbed off the safety, and marched through the Pullman kitchen to the back door. As far as she could tell, the yard was empty, its grass long since given over to weeds and bare earth.

Still . . .

A low, constant hissing.

Shit, she thought; she had left the outside faucet on. That's what it was—water spilling onto the weeds beneath the damn faucet. She tried to remember when she last was out here, and couldn't. Good God, it could have been as long as a week, maybe more. Her water bill was going to be—

She laughed and shook her head.

Who cared about a stupid water bill? She

wasn't going to be around to pay it anyway. Nevertheless, a twinge of guilt at all that waste made her open the door and step outside, swinging immediately to the right and crouching under the kitchen window. She already had her hand on the faucet when she realized it was dry.

No water.

"What the hell?"

The noise grew louder, and now she heard what she thought was whispering.

She rose and turned in the same move.

Too terrified to scream, she managed to fire twice before she was struck and spun away from the house, her arms flailing, her clothes shredded, strips of flesh taken and flung against the wall, her eyes blinded, her lips gone.

When it was over, she remained on her feet for as long as it took for a breeze to touch her.

When she fell, no one heard her.

Lanaya folded his napkin beside his empty plate. "If it's all right with you, I'll pick you up in the morning. The sooner we get there, the sooner we can leave."

Mulder reached for a glass of water. "You don't sound very proud of your home."

"It's for your own good, Agent Mulder. And there's not much to see." He pushed his chair back, but neither Mulder nor Scully moved. "I have to admit, I'm still not convinced you're looking in the right place. Coincidence, that's all it is."

"Maybe. Probably, if you like. But as I already said to someone, we have no choice."

"Sure, no problem. I understand."

Mulder turned around, looking for a waiter to signal so he could get the check. Who he saw was Sheriff Sparrow coming through the front door. By his attitude, the way he snapped a question at the clerk, who had walked over to greet him, it was business. Bad business.

"Scully," he said quietly, and excused himself to hurry into the lobby.

Sparrow brushed the clerk aside with a brusque nod and stared over Mulder's shoulder. "News," he said.

"What?"

"Lanaya been with you all this time?"

Mulder nodded. "What's happened?"

"You already eat?"

"Sheriff, would you mind telling me what's going on?"

Sparrow stared, shook himself without moving a muscle, and blew out a sigh. "Sorry. I didn't mean to snap like that. But I guess you're in luck, Agent Mulder. There's been another one."

Mulder beckoned to Scully automatically as he said, "Who?"

"Donna Falkner."

*   *   *

Shots, two, maybe three, the sheriff told them as he sped out of the parking lot. A neighbor went over to complain, couldn't get an answer at the front door and wandered around to the back. As soon as he saw the body, he called the sheriff's office. As soon as the first deputy saw the body, he called the sheriff, knowing the FBI was in on this case.

Several patrol cars were already on the scene when they arrived, and an ambulance backed into the driveway. Yellow crime scene ribbon fluttered around the property. A handful of people stood in the lot across the street.

"How well did you know her?" Mulder asked as Sparrow led them around the garage to the back.

"She was a pain in the ass." A sharp wave. "She was okay, though."

"Did you know she was going on vacation?"

Sparrow stopped and turned at the corner. "Are you crazy? She never went on vacation. Working herself to death is what she was. Wanted to be a goddamn millionaire before she was thirty-five."

Mulder stepped around him and walked slowly through the shin-high weeds. A sheet had been placed over the body. He didn't bother to ask if the ME had been called; this report wouldn't be any different from the others.

Scully brushed by him and knelt beside the sheet. He stood behind her, holding his breath as she pulled on a pair of latex gloves, pinched a corner, and pulled it back.

Mulder looked away.

Scully braced herself on the ground with one hand, and whispered something he couldn't catch. He saw a shudder work its way down her back before she asked if someone had a camera. A deputy appeared at her side, and she directed the lens as she pulled the sheet farther back.

The mutilation here wasn't as complete as the others. There were areas where the skin was raw but still intact, and areas where a gleam of white showed through liquid red. Her face, however, was completely gone, as was most of her hair.

This had not been a swift dying.

While the sheriff barked and grumbled at his men, Mulder began a slow walk around the yard, until he realized that the color near and on the ground was actually bits of flesh. So were the splotches on the wall near an outside spigot. At the foundation just below it, he found the gun, took a pen from his pocket and picked it up through the trigger guard. Two shots, maybe three, the neighbor had said.

At what?

"Scully."

She looked up, a little pale but recovered.

He jerked his head to tell her he would be inside when she was finished, then opened the kitchen door and went in.

It was still hot, no moving air, and no sign that she intended to return from wherever it was she'd been heading. The drawers in the tiny bedroom dresser were empty; there were a few cartons in the spare room, which looked like those he'd seen in the Cherokee outside. Nothing in the medicine cabinet. Papers and some ledgers in the desk; bills paid and unpaid, but no letters.

He didn't realize how much sunlight had slipped away until someone snapped on an overhead light.

It didn't make the place look any better.

When he took another turn around the room, he saw a briefcase against the wall beside the desk. He knelt, lifted it up, and raised an eyebrow in mild surprise. It was heavier than it looked.

When he opened it, he knew why.

"What do you know?" he said softly, closed it again, and snapped the locks. He kept it in his hand as he went through the house again, finding nothing more than tangles of dust in the corners.

Eventually he found himself by the window, staring at Nick Lanaya, who stood by a pickup parked across the street. Funny reaction, he thought as he headed for the door. The man's partner is murdered, and he just stands there.

He moved onto the stoop and waved, but Lanaya didn't see him.

He was too busy talking to Leon Ciola.

SEVENTEEN

X "Mulder."

He lifted a hand to his shoulder, bringing Scully out of the house and cautioning her at the same time. He pointed when she stood beside him.

"Well, well."

The two men were close together, sideways to the house, every so often glancing down into the truck's bed. Not once did they show any interest in the deputies bustling around the area, or in the police when they arrived, lights spinning. Mulder couldn't tell if they were arguing or not, but they certainly weren't simply passing the time.

He could see Ciola's shark smile; he couldn't read Lanaya's face at all.

Then Ciola jabbed Lanaya's chest with a stiff finger, once, twice, and leaned so close their noses almost touched.

"Do you think we should join them?" Scully asked.

"What, and disturb their grief?" He sidestepped back into the living room. "Look at this, Scully." He set the briefcase on the desk and opened it to show her the packets of money he had found, as many as could be crammed in without bursting the seams.

"A bank is safer." She picked up a packet, another, but there was no sense trying to fix the amount now. Some were in equal amounts, others were mixed. That there was thousands, however, was beyond question. She pulled back her hand and closed the briefcase with a slap. "The same as the others, Mulder." Her gloves had already been stripped off, but she scrubbed her hands anyway. "Not as complete, but the same." She looked at him, almost angry. "I'm going to do this autopsy myself. And this time the report will be right."

"What will it say, Agent Scully?" Nick Lanaya asked from the doorway.

She turned to him. "It will say, once the remains have been confirmed, that Donna Falkner was murdered by person or persons unknown, for one thing. For another, it will say that it appears to be in the same manner of death as the others you've had in this area." She turned away. "You'll have to wait for the rest."

Lanaya sagged against the door frame, head bowed. "I looked in the Cherokee."

Mulder kept the case as he walked over to Lanaya. "She was your partner. Where was she going with all that?"

Lanaya didn't look up. "I would say she was stealing it. According to the markings, they should have been sold months ago." Suddenly he kicked back at the screen door, slamming it against the house. "Goddamnit, Mulder, what the hell was she doing? All the years we worked together—" He kicked the door again and stared blindly into the room.

This time Mulder saw the pain. And something else. Maybe betrayal.

He nudged Lanaya until he went outside, and they walked away from the house, Mulder drawing closer until the man had no conscious choice but to take him to the truck.

The bed was empty, except for a length of tarp folded near the cab.

"I didn't know you knew Leon," Mulder said, careful to keep accusation from his voice.

"There isn't an adult Konochine alive who doesn't know all the others, Agent Mulder. You can hardly avoid it the way we live."

"It seemed a bit more than just casual, from what I saw."

"Personal, okay? It was personal." Lanaya's expression couldn't decide whether to be angry or insulted. "I was with you, remember?" A one-sided, humorless smile flashed on, flashed off. "Just in case you were wondering."

"I wasn't. I have a pretty good short-term memory. Do you happen to know where Mr. Ciola was?"

"Don't know, don't give a shit." Lanaya reached into the bed and picked up a twig with long needles on it. He twirled it between his fingers before flicking it away. "Stupid woman. My God, what . . . what . . ." He gave up.

"You were lovers?"

The Indian shrugged, one shoulder. "For a while. A couple of years back. Turned out we wanted to be business partners more, so we stopped."

"That briefcase is filled with money. Would you have any idea where she got it?"

Radio chatter hung over the street.

A cop and a deputy laughed too loudly.

It should be dark, Mulder thought as he waited for an answer, there's too much light here. It should be dark.

"We haven't been doing too well lately, actually," Lanaya finally admitted. He sniffed, rubbed his nose with the back of a hand, and pushed his hat up off his forehead. "About a year ago, she said the usual stuff wasn't working anymore, that we needed a gimmick, something to distinguish our product from all the other Indian stuff getting produced around here." He laughed bitterly. "I got a bad feeling, Agent Mulder. A bad feeling I've been had." Another laugh, and he slapped the truck's side. "Son of a bitch! When they find out about this, I'll never be able to get them to trust me again."

Scully and Sparrow left the house, talking softly.

Lanaya swept a nervous hand back over his hair several times. "Will I . . . she has no relatives, I mean. Will I have to, you know, identify her?"

"That won't be necessary."

He looked, one eye nearly closed. "That bad?"

Mulder couldn't face him. "There'll have to be the usual tests."

"Tests?" He moved as if to take a run at the house. "Tests? Then how the hell do you know it's her, Mulder? My God, maybe it's someone else, a vagrant or something."

The only thing he could say was, "I know, Mr. Lanaya. I don't want to, but you'll have to trust me on this. I know it's her."

Lanaya made a growling noise in his throat, took a step around the truck, and asked with a look if he was needed. Mulder waved him on, and backed away back when the pickup barreled away, turning the corner without the brake lights flaring.

Mulder watched for a moment, then returned to the front yard, where Scully joined him.

"You all right?" he asked, seeing the expression on her face.

She nodded. "I'm just finding it a little hard to believe, that's all." She glanced toward the house. "Aside from the method, though, it's strange."

"That's not strange enough?"

She almost smiled. "Did you get a good look at the yard?"

"I saw the bare patch where she fell, if that's what you mean."

"Right. But before we leave, take another look. That bare area where the grass and weeds were cut down, that wasn't done by any kind of mower I'm aware of."

"Wait."

She passed a hand over her chin. "What I mean is, where she died isn't where she was first attacked. Whoever killed her . . . it's as if she was pushed around, and the murderer followed her."

"A force like that, I'm not surprised. When you get into a fight, you hardly ever stick to one place."

"This wasn't like a fistfight, Mulder. She wasn't punched around, falling down and getting up again. From what I can tell, given the . . . given the positions of the body, and the flesh and bone shards around the yard, she fell only once. When she died."

Mulder swallowed, but said nothing.

"The point is, Mulder—whoever attacked

her, with whatever weapon, kept her on her feet."

"But the force it would take to do that much damage . . . " He gestured toward the house.

"Exactly, Mulder," she said. "Exactly. She should have fallen almost immediately. But she didn't."

That night, after the paperwork was done, interviews completed, and he and Sheriff Sparrow had finished debriefing each other, he returned to the bench in the garden. His room had grown too small, and Scully was transcribing her notes into the computer. Her mind was already on the morning autopsy—a fresh, puzzling corpse to decipher.

Oh God, he thought; you're sick, pal, you're really sick. What you need is a vacation.

He almost laughed.

Right; that's what got me into this in the first place.

The Rio Grande was higher after the downpour, but only slightly, and the ground and paths were completely dry. There were no strolling guests tonight, either; that didn't surprise him. Word was probably out that the killer had struck again. For a night or two, people would stick close to home, the papers would editorialize about the alarming incidence of psychopathic murders in contemporary society, and someone, somewhere, would manage to reap a large or small political harvest.

Which knowledge got him exactly nowhere.

He reached down between his legs and picked up a pebble. He bounced it on his palm a few times before swatting it toward the water.

He did it a second time, swinging a little harder.

He stood for the third one, and hit it with a fist. It stung a knuckle, but he barely felt it. It was the motion that mattered. When he missed the fourth stone, he considered stopping wasting time and going back to the room. That lasted as long as it took him to find it, and miss again.

Now it was a matter of personal honor, and now he couldn't find the damn thing. Not that any of the others he spotted while on his hands and knees wouldn't have worked, but the one he had missed was the one he wanted.

He was nearly stretched out under the bench, feeling like a jackass, when he heard the rustle of something moving through the brush on the riverbank. At first he thought it might be the evening breeze, but listening for a few seconds told him it was too irregular.

Stop and start.

Just out of reach of the tree lamps and the moonlight, and the lamp poles along the bank.

He used the bench to push himself to his feet,

staring upriver as he dusted off his knees. That, too, was a waste of time; the lamps in front of him blocked any chance of seeing what lay beyond.

The rustling stopped.

All right, so what do they have around here at night? Dogs, cats, coyotes? After that, he went blank.

When he heard it again, he took a long step off the path and picked up a small rock, aimed, and threw it as hard as he could. The crash of the missile through the brush and weeds was followed by the dull plop of its landing in shallow water. But there was no yelp, no sudden rush of an animal scurrying to get away.

Nothing at all, in fact; nothing at all.

Accepting that as a sign he was in danger of losing it, he flicked one more pebble at the water and started back to his room. He hadn't gone three steps when the noise returned.

Not a rustling now, but a barely audible hissing.

Not stop and start, but continuous and moving; slowly, very slowly.

Common sense and experience ordered him to head immediately for the inside, or, at the very least, get Scully out here with him.

What he did, for no good reason he could think of, was sidestep cautiously off the path, turning his head in short stages to try to pinpoint the source's location, whatever the source was. When he reached the lamp poles, his right hand closed around one as he slipped past, while his left instinctively slipped his gun from its holster.

He wouldn't have done that if he hadn't heard the whispering.

More than one voice, although he couldn't tell how many. Nor could he understand what they were saying. One moment it sounded like muffled laughter, the next like little children exchanging secrets in the dark.

Beyond the last pole, there was still several yards of cleared earth straight ahead, while to the left the ground sloped downward toward the river. He flexed his knees to keep his balance on the slope, to keep from sliding as he moved forward, staring, silently cursing the weak reach of the lamplight. He could barely see the brush, could only just make out a twisted branch above it, no higher than his head.

The noise was on the other side, coming toward him.

Carefully he reached behind him, fumbled for and grabbed the last square pole, an clumsy position until he put most of his weight on his right foot.

The whispering sounded more frantic, quickly blending into what sounded like a low hum.

No animal, he knew; and he couldn't see how it could be people, either. That many would make a different kind of noise, and it certainly would be louder. Which made his drawn weapon a little ludicrous.

If there was nothing to shoot at, why have it out?

But nothing didn't make a noise.

It didn't hiss.

It didn't whisper.

He released the lamp pole and eased forward, keeping low, freezing when he had a sudden image of a woman about to open a door everyone in the theater knew hid the monster. They called her stupid, they yelled at her not to do it, they threw things at the screen to get her attention, but she opened it anyway.

And she was always wrong.

And what, he asked himself, does that make you?

Hissing, climbing to a higher pitch that puzzled him because the pitch was still quite low.

It reminded him of something.

It definitely reminded him of something.

He took a step back, snapping his head around when something splashed to his left. No ripples that he could see, not even when he heard another splash, farther across the water. He could have turned then, but he didn't want to show his back to whatever was out there. He wanted to see it if he could, just in case it came into the open and could see him, too.

Then something struck the pole, taking a chip from the edge.

He didn't wait to see if it had been a shot; he fired one of his own into the dark, whirled and began to run, slipping once on the grass, flinging a hand out to stop him from falling on his chest.

When he reached the bench, he turned, trotting backward, staring at something he could finally see down by the lamps.

He never had a chance to see it clearly.

He heard a voice, heard a popping sound, and all the lamps turned red.

EIGHTEEN

X Dugan Velador was tired of being old. He didn't want to die, that would be a waste of his life. What he wanted, however, was for people to stop coming to him with questions whose answers they already knew if they would only stop to think. What he wanted was a little peace, and he didn't think that was too selfish a wish. Not at his age. Not after all he had done for his people.

He also wanted the killing to stop.

It should have ended the other night, the last night in the kiva.

For as long as he could remember, and for all that he had been taught and told, the last night

195

should have meant the end, for it had always been before.

Not this time.

This time, from what he had heard on the portable radio he kept by his bed, another one had died. A woman. The name was familiar. He couldn't place the face or the occasion of the meeting, so he knew she wasn't Konochine *frastera,* one of those who had left.

Still, the name was familiar, and he worried at it while he ate breakfast, worried at it while, with a sitting blanket over one shoulder, he walked from his place to sleep by the Tribal Center to the Wall that overlooked the road that pointed west. When he was younger, but not young by any calculation, he used to sit there every dawn and stare at the unseen place where he knew Annie lived.

He tried to will her to return.

He prayed for her to leave the ranch and move back to her rightful home.

When that didn't work, he figured he had either really garbled the prayers so badly that the spirits hadn't recognized them, or he wasn't half as strong as he thought he was. Velador was a practical man. When one thing didn't work, there was always something else. If the spirits wouldn't listen, someone else would.

As Nick would say, what the hell.

The only thing he hadn't done, and would not

do, was visit her in person. That would insult her, and demean him.

Practical, however, sometimes meant taking a bite out of pride, swallowing it, and hoping it wasn't poison.

He would have to think about it hard today. The killing of the woman he could not remember was too important. Annie would know that; maybe she already did. Maybe she would take a bite, too, and at least meet him halfway.

If she didn't, he'd be sitting in the sun for nothing.

Practical didn't always mean that what he did was smart.

When Mulder opened his eyes, he instantly allowed as how he fully deserved the booming explosion whose echoes rebounded through his skull for what seemed like forever. And when forever arrived, he still had a splitting headache.

At least he was still in his room, or would be as soon as the walls stopped shifting.

Last night, when he'd regained consciousness, he had thought he was in a hospital. A beautiful hospital with soft lights and attractive, natural decorations complete with all the appropriate scents and aromas. The bed was too hard, though, and the air conditioning had been turned up way too high. They hadn't even bothered to cover him with a blanket.

When his vision cleared an eyeblink later, he realized someone had stretched him out on one of the benches in the motel's back garden.

Scully knelt beside him, urging him to stop hiding and come all the way out. When he did, she scolded him for doing whatever he had done to get himself clunked like this.

"Clunked?"

He had tried to sit up, but his head wouldn't let him; neither would his stomach. A rolling nausea engulfed him briefly, and he tightened his jaw, clenched his fists until the urge to vomit had passed.

Sparrow leaned into sight then, and between thumb and forefinger held up a stone that would fit perfectly in his palm. He turned it so Mulder could see the fresh bloodstain.

"What were you doing, Mulder?" Scully's expression was stern, but her voice was pure concern.

Again he tried to sit up, and again the dizziness was too strong. He accepted the order her hand on his shoulder gave him. "Someone was out there." He pointed vaguely, not sure of the right direction. "Maybe more than one. Definitely more than one." His eyes closed as he tried to remember.

While he did, the sheriff said, "And they knocked you out with a rock? Agent Scully said she heard a shot."

Voices had interrupted them, for which he had

been grateful. He needed time for all parts of him to get back together, and when they did, reluctantly, he said, "No, never mind. I don't think it was a person."

The sheriff grunted. "Then you're the first man on record to get himself beaned by a coyote."

"Not an animal either."

"He's delirious." Sparrow sounded disgusted. "Such a little scratch, too. I'll be back in the morning, folks. There's nothing out there, Agent Scully. And if there was, he's long gone by now. Long gone."

More voices, footsteps, murmuring, then silence.

He opened his eyes.

Scully was still there, patient. "What did you shoot at, Mulder?"

"Little scratch? I thought a boulder hit me."

"Mulder, pay attention. What did you shoot at?"

He hadn't known then, and he didn't know now. Not that he could think very straight yet anyway, even if he did know. Fingers touched his forehead gingerly, skated over it until they reached the lump of a square bandage just above his left temple. He pressed, it protested, and he let the hand fall away.

What the hell was it?

Sleep on it, he ordered, and no one argued.

When he next woke up, the ache had lessened considerably, and he felt well enough to stumble into the bathroom before his bladder exploded. A double palmful of water scattered the rest of the cobwebs, allowing him to check his reflection without wanting to break the mirror.

All in all, he looked a lot better than he felt. The bandage was small, and someone, probably Scully, had already washed the blood from his face. Other than his hair poking out in all directions, he figured he looked pretty human.

A few minutes of washing, holding onto the basin while ripples of nausea and dizziness settled, and getting that hair back into place, and he felt even better. Hungry, even. He was about to give Scully a call to meet him for a late breakfast when he spotted a note taped to the mirror over the low dressing table in the front room. It was a reminder that she had an autopsy to perform, and a warning not to do anything on his own. She hoped to be back by noon, or shortly after.

Taking care to move without jarring anything loose inside his skull, he finished dressing and stepped outside.

The sky was blindingly blue, the sun simply blinding, and the heat hadn't changed, although it might have been, relatively, a bit cooler than yesterday. None of it did his head any good, and he hurried to the restaurant and the safety of the indoors.

A simple breakfast eaten in solitude allowed him to get past the muted throbbing behind his brow, to go over what had happened the night before.

Not that he needed much reminding. The humiliation of the lump was bad enough.

What had happened was, he had ignored all his instincts and had opened that damn door. What had made him do it, he couldn't figure out. It had been more than simple curiosity, and until the end of the episode, he didn't recall feeling all that threatened.

So . . . why?

He ordered a second tall glass of orange juice and sipped it while he watched the other guests come and go, wind through the courtyard, take pictures of each other beneath the cottonwood. In the white sun they had no idea what he had seen yesterday in that weed-infested yard; or if they did, they weren't going to let it ruin their day. A tale to tell when they got home, nothing more, a whole lot less.

The glass was empty when he remembered something else—that the noise he had heard by the river had reminded him of something. He concentrated, and scowled in defeat when he couldn't give it a name. He did bring back the feeling, however, and it made him put the glass down and take a deep calming breath.

Above and in that hissing was the whispering.

she is special, mr. mulder.

His spine stiffened.

she hears the wind.

He was on his feet before he realized he had even left his seat, and that he hadn't yet received his check. Luckily, the waiter spotted him and came right over. Mulder signed it, added a large tip and an effusive verbal thanks that startled the young man, and did his best not to run from the room to the lobby reception desk. There were no messages from Scully, and none from Sheriff Sparrow, who had said, Mulder recalled, that he would be back sometime this morning to ask some questions about last night.

He wondered if he could convince the man that he hadn't been delirious at all.

The wind.

Not wanting to confine himself to his room again, he strolled deliberately slowly around the courtyard, for all the world like a tourist who couldn't think of a damn thing to do. When he couldn't stand it anymore, he veered into the passageway to the back garden. Except for a woman standing near the center, he was alone.

The wind.

As he passed her, heading for the place where he'd been struck, he heard a noise. A familiar noise. One that made him stop, that made his headache return.

"Are you all right?"

The woman, a short Hispanic woman in a maid's uniform, looked up at him, not really concerned; she was only being polite because she had to. Behind her he saw a wheeled cart stacked with fresh linens and towels.

He nodded, and stared at her hands when the noise started again.

"Hey," she said, both a question and a warning.

"I'm sorry." He added a smile to the apology and moved on, forcing himself not to look back. A moment later he heard the cart's wheels roll quickly across the stone. Obviously she thought he was nuts. Maybe he was. The sound he had just heard was an emery board being drawn across her nail. Almost like sandpaper.

At the bench where he had been last night, he looked toward the spot where he had heard the hissing, the whispers.

He didn't have to go there now to know what he would find, but he went anyway. A justification, a confirmation. He hadn't seen it on the riverbank where Paulie Deven had been killed, but he had seen it yesterday, in Donna Falkner's backyard. He just hadn't known what he had been looking at.

It didn't take long.

At the place where the grass met the underbrush, he stopped and rose up slightly on his toes. The growth wasn't so dense that he couldn't get in there; he didn't need to. He could see well enough from where he stood.

About ten feet away was an open spot, a scar.

The branches of the brush at its rim were either snapped off or had their bark worn through. Stretching his neck allowed him a glimpse of the ground, and the debris that covered it.

He grinned.

"Agent Mulder!"

Sheriff Sparrow came into the garden, and Mulder answered him with a gesture that he'd be there in a second. One more scan of the area showed him everything he needed to see, and he rubbed his hands briskly as he returned to the garden path.

"Sheriff, do you think you can get hold of Nick Lanaya?"

"I suppose so. What do you need?"

Scully, he thought as he headed for the sheriff, you're going to hate what I know.

You're going to hate it a lot.

NINETEEN

X There were no chairs in the lobby. The only place to sit was a thick wood bench beside the fountain. Mulder waited while Sparrow used the desk phone to reach Lanaya, hoping that Scully would return soon. He didn't want to leave without her, but he felt a need to move fast, before someone else died.

After last night, he had more than an unpleasant feeling that he knew who that target was.

Sparrow sat beside him, hat and sunglasses off, rubbing his eyes. "I left a message. There's only a couple of phones out there. Portable jobs like you have. Half the time they're left behind." He leaned back against the fountain's broad lip. "So you want to tell me what's going on, or is this going to be one of those need-to-know bullshit things?"

Mulder shook his head. "No need-to-know, Sheriff. Scully and I are going to need all the help we can get." He checked the time, wondering aloud how long his partner would be.

"She's done, and on her way," the man said wryly.

"How do you know that?"

"I read minds, Mulder." The jerk of a thumb toward the reception desk. "Plus, I called."

Close, Mulder thought; not quite, but close enough.

"Half an hour, maybe a little more." The sheriff rocked to nudge Mulder with a shoulder. "I can't read minds that good."

Mulder debated. No matter how many times he told it, there would be arguments and counter-suggestions, especially from Scully. He decided it would be best to get it out in one session rather than have to keep repeating himself.

It would also give him time to convince himself more thoroughly that he was right.

At his hesitation, the sheriff took off his hat and dropped it beside him on the bench. He took a notepad from his breast pocket, and a pen whose tip had been chewed close to chipping. "Okay. So how about you tell me about last night? You fired a gun, Mulder. FBI or not, that needs some explanation."

Grateful for the change of subject, Mulder complied readily. He took the man through his movements step by step from the time he entered the garden until he had been struck. Sparrow asked few questions. A clarification here, a doubt there. When Mulder was done, the man put the notepad away, fixed the pen to his pocket, and scratched his forehead.

"Basically, what you're telling me is that you shot at a shadow."

"No, Sheriff. I shot at something that was definitely no shadow."

"So what was it?"

Mulder smiled and stood. "Patience is a virtue, Sheriff Sparrow."

"Patience, my friend, is a royal pain in the ass. And you gotta admit, I've been pretty damn patient with you."

Mulder agreed, and decided to take the lawman out back to show him what he had found. Sparrow reminded him that he had already been there, he and his men, but Mulder insisted gently. What he wanted the sheriff to see was something his men, good as they were, probably wouldn't have thought twice about.

"I did the same, Sheriff, the first time I saw it."

They were already at the riverbank when Scully called his name.

He made a silent wish for no surprises, no complications, then looked at the sheriff.

Sparrow was laughing.

"What?"

He pointed at Scully, then reached over and tapped a finger against Mulder's chest. "Couldn't stand it, could you?"

That was the first time Mulder realized that in dressing this morning, he had put on his tie and blue suit. It had been automatic. He had been too busy fighting his headache to think. His hands had grabbed what they knew best.

Scully, too, was the same.

For some reason, even out here, she looked more natural that way.

"Well?" he asked.

Scully greeted the sheriff almost curtly, pushed at her hair to keep the steady breeze from blinding her, and said, "Mulder, I do not want to have to do that again, ever."

"I'd think," Sparrow said, "you'd be used to it by now. Cutting them up, I mean, figuring things out."

"You don't get used to it," she told him. "You just find a way not to let it bother you for a while." She grabbed a folded paper from her shoulder bag, glanced at it, and took a deep breath. "You'll be pleased to know there are no surprises, Mulder. And Dr. Rios was right—it wasn't skinning and it wasn't flaying. Scouring, for the time being, is a pretty damn good word."

"What killed her?"

"Simply? Layman's terms? Shock. If you want the details, we can start with the near-total destruction of a major organ—which is what the skin is—coupled with rapid fluid loss from various sources, including—"

"Never mind," the sheriff interrupted, a queasy look on his face. "I get the picture."

"No," she contradicted. "I don't think you do. Mulder, there were particles of sandy dirt lodged in the sinuses and eye sockets. And in the brain."

"What the hell could do something like that?" Sparrow demanded.

"Force," Mulder answered. "A lot of force." He started for the river. "Which is why I want you to take a look at this."

Scully looked at him quizzically. "What?"

"Just look, Scully. I'll explain on our way to the Mesa."

She didn't argue, but followed the sheriff to the brush at the edge of the grass, where Mulder pointed out the cleared area farther on. It took a while until they found a way through without ripping themselves to shreds, and when they reached the rough circle, he broke off an already damaged twig and held it up.

"The bark," he said. "Torn off."

The ground at their feet was littered with shredded leaves and shards of twigs and branches.

"If I didn't know better," Sparrow said, "I'd say

a nut with a weed-whacker got roaring drunk in here."

"There's the same sort of damage done over at Donna Falkner's house," Mulder told them as they made their way back to the garden. "I saw it, but because the yard was so badly kept, it didn't hit me until this morning."

Sparrow told them to meet him in the parking lot; he'd go in to see if Lanaya had been reached. Scully walked with her head down, every few steps shaking her head. Then she stopped Mulder with a touch. "A device, maybe? Maybe the sheriff wasn't so far off with that weed-trimmer idea." She looked away, looked back. "But that doesn't explain the dirt. Just falling wouldn't do it."

"No, you're right."

He started for the car, but she blocked him, a hand briefly on his chest. "What is it, Mulder? What are you up to?"

"Sangre Viento," he answered. "It's the only thing that makes sense."

"Really?" She glanced over at the sheriff, hurrying toward them. "And you think that makes sense?"

"It does to me."

"Of course it does," she said flatly. "Whatever was I thinking of."

"Nick's waiting at the res," Sparrow said, herding them toward his cruiser. A hard look at

Mulder. "We'll ride together, all right? I want to hear this. Just tell me I'm gonna like it."

Mulder couldn't, and by his expression the sheriff knew it. He rolled his eyes in resignation and wondered aloud how Scully put up with it.

"Patience," Mulder said as he slid into the back-seat.

"Pain in the ass," the sheriff answered.

"Maybe. But I've gotten used to it."

Scully wasn't amused.

Nick hunkered down beside the old man, hands draped across his knees. "You're going to bake out here, Dugan."

The old man only shrugged.

"The FBI is coming."

"There was a death."

"I know."

"The woman. I think I know her."

Nick shifted uneasily. "Donna Falkner, Dugan. She's . . . was my partner."

"Ah, yes. I remember her now. She ran pretty good."

Nick couldn't help but smile. "Yes, she did. And she helped us a lot. I hope you remember that, too."

The old man brushed invisible sand from his blanket, the only admission Nick was likely to get.

"There should not have been a killing, Nick."

"Yes. I know that."

"There should not have been any killings." Dugan's head turned stiffly. "The cattle sometimes. I remember a coyote once. But no people, Nick. Never any people before."

Nick nodded earnestly, leaning as close as he could without toppling into the old man's lap. "That's what I've been trying to tell you, Dugan. If we don't do something, the FBI will find out, and we won't be able to stop the news people or the police or anybody from trampling all over the Mesa." He lowered his voice. "But if we stop him now, there'll be nothing to see. Nothing to find."

A breeze stirred the grass.

"Dugan. Father. The Falkner woman won't be the last to die. You know that."

The old man's head bowed, his hands gathering in his lap. "I am hoping for—"

Nick couldn't help himself; he grabbed the man's shoulder harshly. "Damnit, she isn't coming back, Dugan. Annie isn't coming back, and she's not going to help." He felt the shoulder stiffen, and snatched his hand away. "If we're going to make it through this, we have to see that Leon is . . ."

He didn't finish.

He didn't have to.

All he could do was wait for Velador to make

up his mind. As he stood, the old man began a low murmuring, and Nick walked away.

He hadn't gone ten paces when the old man said, "Nick," just loud enough to hear.

He turned to face Dugan's back, and the right hand raised, finger pointing to the sky.

"The FBI."

"What about them?"

"They must be stopped."

The breeze blew.

The sand stirred.

Imagine, Mulder said, a group of men, extremely devout men, confined for so long in a single room. The kiva. Imagine, as he had already mentioned to Scully, the energy they must create and radiate as they perform the rituals required of their faith. Suppose, then, there are moments during that time when the energy can no longer be confined, but its excess escapes through the hole in the ceiling. It can dissipate. Maybe someone nearby feels a little discomfort, but nothing more. They might blame it on the wind.

But suppose, just suppose, it doesn't scatter. Suppose it gathers instead. Suppose it concentrates.

Suppose the earliest Konochine knew this. They would also know that such a concentration would be potentially dangerous. So they come to the valley within the Wall from wherever they had been, and make it their home. It's isolated, protected by both the hills and the mountains, and nobody—not the other tribes, not the Spanish, not the whites—bothers them for very long.

But the energy is the important thing.

What happens to it?

Sangre Viento.

Blood Wind.

Nando making a spinning motion with his hand.

He called it a whirlwind.

Not a tornado dropping from a cloud; an extraordinary dust devil, rising from the ground.

It spins alone in the desert, and when the energy is used, it falls apart, just like disturbing the plane of an ordinary dust devil will cause it to collapse. It's reasonable to suppose, then, that once in a while an animal gets caught in it, and because it spins at such high speeds, far faster than an ordinary dervish, and because it's made up of gritty, sandy earth, leaves, twigs, whatever else is on the ground . . .

Imagine, he said.

Imagine the power.

TWENTY

He stared at the passing desert, elbow on the armrest, one hand curled lightly across his chin. Now that he had said it aloud, heard his voice, he knew he was right. There was no baroque device a murderer could cart around with him, and there was no group of whip-wielding maniacs.

Sangre Viento was all there was.

And one thing more.

"Mulder," Scully said in that voice he had heard so many times before, "assuming, and only assuming, for the moment that you're right—"

Sheriff Sparrow grumbled a few words, most of which were "bullshit."

Mulder couldn't miss the tone of disappointment and disbelief.

"—what you're talking about is . . ." She faltered. "Is a form of undirected psychic, for want of a better word, energy. Assuming it's true," she added hastily. "But how does that random activity explain four people dying? It seems to me that where and when they died indicates something else entirely."

"Premeditation," he said, still watching the desert.

"Exactly."

"Oh, sweet Jesus," Sparrow snapped. "Are you telling me there's somebody who can aim this thing? Assuming," he said sarcastically, "you're right." He yanked the cruiser so hard off the interstate, Mulder nearly fell over. "For God's sake, gimme a break."

Unfortunately, Mulder couldn't see any other answer. What he could see, however, was a couple of names who might be interested in such control. The question was, why would they feel the need to kill?

"I mean," the sheriff continued, working himself into a self-righteous rage, "how can a couple of intelligent people like you believe in such crap? Bunch of old Indians sitting around a campfire, shooting cosmic something-or-other at each other? You been nibbling at some peyote or what?" He slapped the steering wheel hard.

"Scully, you're a doctor, for God's sake. You gonna tell me you actually go along with this shit?"

Mulder held his breath.

"Sheriff," she answered in her most official, neutral voice, "I have never known Mulder to be so far off-base that I would dismiss everything he says out of hand."

"Ah . . . crap."

Thank you, Scully, Mulder thought with a brief smile, I'd rather have a resounding "absolutely and how dare you," but that'll do in a pinch.

On the other hand, the day that "absolutely and how dare you" actually came, it would probably kill him with amazement.

They passed the Double-H, and he wondered if any of this had touched Annie. He wondered what she had heard on the wind. Whatever it was, he didn't believe for a second she was in any way involved.

Suddenly the sheriff braked hard, and Mulder shot his hand out to brace himself against the seatback. In the road ahead, a pickup had been parked across the lane. Nick Lanaya lounged against the bed, arms folded across his chest.

"Stupid bastard," the sheriff muttered. "Has everyone gone nuts on me today?"

They climbed out slowly, Mulder moving around the car to join Scully. As he did, he looked up the boulder-strewn slope on his right and saw a figure sitting near the top, featureless and black against the sky.

"Dugan Velador," Lanaya said, pushing away from the truck. "He's like a priest. One of the six." A tolerant chuckle and a gesture to the hill. "He likes it up there. He says it helps him think."

"But it's so hot," Scully said, astonished. "How does he survive?"

"He's Konochine, Agent Scully. He can pretty much survive anything." He cleared his throat. "So what's up? I got Chuck's message. What can I do for you?"

The sheriff hitched his belt. "Nick, you ain't gonna—"

"We need to see the reservation, Mr. Lanaya," Mulder said, further cutting the sheriff off by standing half in front of him. "There are some questions we have to ask of the people in charge."

"The Council?"

"Are they the priests?" Scully asked.

Lanaya shrugged. "Mostly, yes. But I don't think they'll talk to you."

Mulder smiled. "That's why you're here. To convince them that cooperation in a murder investigation would be the right thing to do. Maybe save some lives."

Lanaya scuffed the ground with the toe of a boot. "Well, to be honest, Agent Mulder, I'm kind of beat today." A sour look at the sheriff. "I spent most of the morning with a police accountant, going over Donna's ledgers and bank account. It seems she was cheating me more than just a little."

"So I gathered."

"Luckily, most of the money is recoverable, so I won't lose much. But it's the shock, you know what I mean? A lot of years I trusted her, and now I'll never know why she did it."

"Your people trusted her, too," Scully said.

"No." He squinted at the hillside. "No, they trusted me. Like I said, I've got a hell of a lot of damage control ahead of me here. And you coming in like this . . . it's only going to make things worse."

Mulder walked over to the truck. "You have air conditioning, right?"

Puzzled, Lanaya nodded.

"Good." He opened the passenger door and beckoned to Scully. "Let's go." Expressionless, Scully climbed in first. "We have a job to do. Right, sheriff?"

All Sparrow could do was nod curtly, and Lanaya shrugged an *it's your funeral* before getting in behind the wheel. But his face was hard, and Mulder saw his fingers tremble as they turned the key to fire the engine. Anger, or nerves.

"Ground rules," Lanaya told them as he maneuvered the pickup around. "You don't get out unless I say it's all right. You don't speak to anyone unless I say it's all right, or they speak to you first. And you sure don't go in any building unless I say it's all right. Okay?"

"Drive, Mr. Lanaya," he said. "Neither one of us has all day."

They drove through the gap, the road curving gently to the right. When the hill was finally behind them, Mulder almost asked him to stop. He wasn't quite sure what he had expected, but it wasn't anything like this.

Off the road to the left were small fields filled with crops. Scattered gunmetal pumps resembling steel dinosaurs worked ceaselessly, pumping well water into an effective series of irrigation ditches. He didn't recognize any of the crops except, in the center and by far the largest field, corn.

It was a stark, surreal contrast to the desert land that surrounded it.

On the right, however, was Sangre Viento Mesa.

Lanaya slowed. "The Place, Agent Mulder. You'll see other mesas, but never one like that."

It rose two hundred vertical feet from the desert floor, its sides ridged and furrowed, and stark. Where sunlight washed it, faint red hinted at iron among the dark tans and browns. There was no green at all. There was no plant life that he could see from this distance. On the flat top were outlines of low buildings. Several large birds circled over it. Its shadow seemed everywhere.

At the north base was the pueblo, and again his vague expectations didn't match the reality.

"Your people weren't cliff dwellers," Scully said softly.

"No. No one has ever lived on the Mesa itself." Lanaya looked at her with a faint smile. "Every so often, maybe once a decade, I'm able to bring in an archaeologist or two and some professors who don't believe it. They insist there have to be cave homes there on several levels, with ladders and all the rest. Like at Puye and Mesa Verde. There aren't."

What there were were neat rows of small abobe houses, a single story each. One, apparently, for each family. All the doors and windows Mulder could see were outlined in pale green. As the road curved closer, he saw laundry hanging from lines on poles, orderly streets in a grid, and at the east end, two larger structures which, Lanaya explained, were a storage building for crops and a tribal center. Incongruously, to Mulder, some of the homes sported television and FM antennas; only a few had vehicles parked beside them, and most of them were pickups. He also spotted a corral where several horses munched on hay and swatted flies with their tails, a trio of black and white dogs trotting along a street, and a low pen populated by chickens whose plumage was almost garish.

It didn't occur to him to think it odd that he couldn't see any litter.

"Where do they work?" Scully asked, leaning as close to the windshield as she could.

"In the fields, in workshops in the center or in their homes. A few go outside, but not many. The Konochine have no unemployment, if that's what you're wondering. You work to eat. You don't work, you don't eat." Lanaya laughed, but not cheerfully. "I don't know of anyone who has ever chosen to starve."

"And your house?" she asked.

Flatly: "You can't see it from here."

Mulder watched a group of white-clothed children playing in front of a building near the pueblo's middle; another group chased each other through the streets, carrying hoops and switches. "What about Leon Ciola?"

Lanaya forced the truck into a tight U-turn and took a short dirt road that led them to the front of the warehouse and the tribal center. No one looked up as he passed except one small boy, whose eyes grew so wide Mulder had to smile.

When the engine stopped, metal creaking, Lanaya opened his door. "Ciola lives where he wants. I don't follow him around, Agent Mulder. He's . . . he's having a difficult time fitting back into the life."

Three steps led to double doors in the center.

Lanaya pushed one open and gestured the others in. "You'll have to ask your questions here."

They were in a large meeting hall with exposed thick beams in the low ceiling. Two doors in the side walls and one in back were closed, their frames painted a pale green. The walls were white. The floor was uncovered. The only decoration was on the back wall over the door, a huge woven tapestry with a depiction of the Mesa in the center. Lightning in the sky. Symbols of sun and moon, of birds and animals. No people at all. Nothing he recognized as a language.

"No one knows how old it is," Lanaya said, his voice low. "My grandfather once told me that his grandfather knew an old woman who knew an old woman who helped with the design." He shrugged. "It doesn't matter."

Against the left wall was a long table of Spanish oak, with equally bulky chairs arranged around it. He led them over and bade them sit, Mulder with his back to the wall, Scully opposite him. "You'll want to talk to one of the Council," he said. "Dugan would be the best."

"The man on the hill?" Mulder said.

"Yes. It's time he came in out of the sun anyway. He's going to get heatstroke one of these days. Wait here. Please. It won't take me long."

The echo of his boots on the floor lingered after he had gone. And once gone, there was no other sound. The outside might as well not have existed.

Scully placed her shoulder bag on the table and folded her hands on it. "He's a strange man, Mulder. One minute you think he hates this place, and then he goes all reverent on you."

"He's been outside. How can you not have a conflict?"

She looked doubtful, but she didn't pursue it. Instead, as he expected, she launched into a perfectly reasonable explanation of why, with his belief in the Sangre Viento, he was pushing the limits of her tolerance. While she grudgingly granted him the possibility of undirected psychic energy—a phrase she nearly choked on— she was not about to grant him deliberate control.

"Do you know what that means?"

"Murder," he answered simply.

"Do you want to try to prove that in court? Do you think Skinner will buy it?"

"Right now, I don't care about Skinner. What I care about is who's doing this." He leaned forward on his arms folded on the table. "Scully, four people are dead, there's one agent missing, every connection points here, or to someone here, and unless we catch him, there's going to be more."

She stared at him for a long time.

He held the stare as long as he could, then sighed and looked down at his blurred reflection in the dark polished wood.

"Ciola," she said then.

He looked up without raising his head.

"Leon Ciola." She slipped a sheet of paper from her bag and slid it over. "You were so busy driving Sheriff Sparrow away with your story that I didn't have a chance to tell you." She tapped the paper with a finger. "Preliminary police report on Donna Falkner's house. A lot of prints were lifted. Hers, of course, and Lanaya's, no surprise, he was her partner. And Leon Ciola's." She cocked an eyebrow. "Some of them in the bedroom."

He glanced over the form and resisted the urge to shout.

"It's hard with only that one conversation," she continued, "but I don't get the feeling that she ran that embezzlement scheme on her own. Ciola could have talked her into it. It's been going on for four years. Two of those years were his last two in prison." Another tap on the paper. "She visited him there, Mulder. Often. Evidently she was the reason he lost his temper in the bar."

Mulder rested his chin on his arm. "She gets greedy. He finds out. His infamous temper."

No answer.

He looked up into a disquieting frown.

"We'll assume again, all right? For the sake of argument?"

He nodded.

"Why Paulie Deven? Why the Constellas?"

He had already thought about that; he already had an answer that disturbed him.

"Practice," he said, lowering his gaze to the table. "All they were to him was practice."

She didn't react, didn't speak. She pulled the paper back, turned it around, and skimmed it. Then she put it back into her bag and let her head rest against the chair's high back. Her lips pursed; her eyes followed an unseen trail on the ceiling.

"He's not one of the Council, Mulder. Ciola—"

"Well, well, well, *chica*," Ciola said from the entrance. "Every time I see you, you can't help but speak my name."

TWENTY-ONE

 Beyond the cornfield, beyond the last of the water pumps, in the desert, the sand began to stir.

With an exaggerated swagger Ciola crossed the hall, swinging his arms, deliberately cracking his heels against the floor for the gunshot sound. His head was bare, his shirt and jeans looked stiff enough to be new, and his hair had been freed from his ponytail to sway against his back as he moved.

"You like it in here?" he asked, spreading his arms.

Neither Mulder nor Scully answered.

He made a face. "This, you know, is the place

where they meet every month. They try to think of a way to banish me, you see?" He laughed and stamped a foot. "I am an embarrassment to them, FBI. I spent a lot of time in the penitentiary, and I think they think this shames them."

He reached the head of the table and dragged the chair back, dropped into it and hooked a leg over the arm.

Scully shifted in her chair to face him, her right arm resting on the table. She said nothing; she only looked.

Ciola gestured toward the entrance. "You're all the talk out there today, Agent Scully, did you know that? It's the red in your hair, I think. I figured you were here to talk to me, is that right? So here I am. So talk."

Scully gave him a little nod. "Where were you yesterday afternoon, Mr. Ciola?"

He shook his head sadly. "You'll have to do better than that. I was telling my parole officer how wonderful it is to be outside again."

"Then how did you know about Donna Falkner? You were there."

"I have a police scanner in my truck." He grinned. "It comes in handy."

"A scanner?" She sounded doubtful.

The grin snapped off. "I'm an Indian, Agent Scully. I'm not a savage."

"You nearly cut a man's head off," Mulder said mildly. "That sounds pretty savage to me."

Ciola only glared at him, a quick glance, before he looked back to Scully. "Anything else?"

"Theft," she said.

The leg slid slowly off the arm. "I kill people, Agent Scully, I don't steal from them. You want a thief, I suggest you have a word with Saint Nick."

"What were you two arguing about? Yesterday. In the street."

"Do you know something, Agent Scully? For the life of me, I can't understand why a woman like you would—"

"Ciola," Mulder said, raising his voice.

The man sighed the sigh of a terribly put-upon man, and looked.

Mulder held up his ID. "Just for the record, the Federal Bureau of Investigation has legal authority on Indian reservations, whether we're asked in or not. That means, Mr. Ciola, that I don't need anyone's permission—not the sheriff's, not your Council's—to bring you in for questioning concerning the murder of Donna Falkner. Or Paulie Deven. Or Matt and Doris Constella." He put the ID back in his pocket. "Why don't you just cut the crap, and answer Agent Scully."

The man looked ready to bolt, and from the corner of her eye, Scully saw Mulder tense for the chase. "He told us it was personal," she said quickly, watching them both relax as if strings had been severed.

"It is."

"How personal?"

"We hate each other, Ms. Scully. I'm an ex-con and he's a saint. I dropped out of high school, he's got degrees up his ass and out his throat." Palms down, he spread his fingers on the table. After a long moment, he said, "How confidential is this? If I tell you something, you put me back in the pen?"

"That depends," Mulder answered.

"On what?"

"On whether I say so," Scully said, holding back a grin at the astonishment on his face.

"Let . . . let me think about it."

"While you're thinking," Mulder said, "tell me how you managed not to be killed by the Sangre Viento."

Ciola gaped, his left hand moving unconsciously to his cheek to brush over the scars. "How the hell did you know that?"

Mulder didn't answer.

Scully knew, however. Now that she could examine them without fearing a knife in her throat, the pattern across his neck and face was clear; at least, clear enough to anyone who knew about the Wind.

"I had a pony," Ciola said quietly. "When I was very little, a man died, one of the six. During the ceremonial, no one leaves the Mesa, or goes into the desert. It's a foolish chance. Only people like Saint Nick do something dumb like that. I was little, and I was foolish, and I wanted my pony. She had broken out of the corral, and I chased her for nearly an hour.

"I almost had her once, but she bolted. I couldn't figure out why until I turned around, and there it was. Right behind me. I fell over backward into an arroyo, and that's what saved me."

Scully couldn't help it: "You believe in this Blood Wind?"

Ciola's fingers fluttered across his face. "That's a stupid question, *chica*. Do you want a stupid answer?"

"No, just a truthful one."

His eyes widened at her boldness, but one of the front doors opened before he had a chance to say a word. Nick Lanaya walked in, an old man trailing behind, both of them unaware of Ciola until they were halfway across the floor.

Lanaya stopped; the old man didn't. He continued on to the table and took the chair on Scully's right.

"What do you want, Leon?" Nick demanded.

"The FBI calls, I answer." He grinned at Mulder. "It's the law, don't you know that?"

"Get out, Leon. They need you in the warehouse."

"Oh, I don't know. There are many questions left to ask." He looked to Scully for support. "They want to know, for example, about Donna. How we loved, how we fought, how we—"

"Chinga!" Lanaya spat, face darkening with rage. "You kill, you dare to come back here as if nothing ever happened, and now you dare to talk—"

"Enough!" Mulder ordered, thumping the table with his fist. "Excuse me," he said to the old man, and turned back to the others. "Mr. Lanaya, for all our sakes, let me or Agent Scully be the ones to decide when Mr. Ciola has told us enough, okay? Mr. Ciola, I take it you're not planning a vacation or anything like that?"

Ciola laughed as he stood. "Don't leave town, eh, *gringo?* Don't worry. I won't. I still have to go to Donna's funeral."

Lanaya grabbed the man's arm as he brushed past him and whispered harshly in his ear. Scully couldn't understand what was said, but it made her wonder when Ciola swallowed heavily and left, nearly at a run. Nick made to follow, but a grunted word from the old man brought him to the table, where he sat in the chair Ciola had just used.

"I'm sorry," he said with a sheepish smile. "The man just drives me crazy." His hand waved in front of his face as if clearing the air of a foul odor. Then he introduced Dugan Velador. "He speaks very good English, so—"

"Have I left, Nick?" Velador asked quietly.

Again Lanaya's face darkened, and he lowered his head and didn't move.

Scully raised an eyebrow to Mulder at the control the old man had, then sat back so she could see both of them at once. She wasn't sure what Mulder wanted her to say, and so deferred to him when he cleared his throat, a signal that he wanted to take charge of the interview for a time.

She hoped, though, that when the Sangre Viento came up, as it surely would, Velador wouldn't be insulted. It would be easy for him to think they were mocking him, or being condescending. And although Nick had warned them of the probability, she was somewhat taken aback when the old man said, "I want you to leave the Mesa now, please. There is nothing here to discuss or tell you."

He stood, the bone necklace he wore rattling softly.

Lanaya stood as well, quickly, but Mulder only clasped his hands on the table and said, "I have reason to believe, Mr. Velador, that someone, probably one of your people, has been using either you, or the six, to establish control of the Sangre Viento." When the old man reached out to grab the edge of the table, Mulder paid him no heed. "If that's true, then this man, sir, has committed four murders, and Agent Scully and I don't intend to leave until we find him, and arrest him."

Well, Scully thought as Velador sank back into his chair, that's certainly being subtle.

* * *

A small leaf danced in a circle in the air, several inches above the ground. From a distance it looked like a butterfly searching for a blossom. Seconds later it was joined by another, this one pierced by a cactus needle.

Below them, the sand began to rise.

Mulder hoped neither the old man nor Scully noticed when he released the breath he'd been holding. Sparring with Ciola had been bad enough, but Velador, whose posture and expression told those who saw him he was meek and too dull to be considered, had given him a start as soon as he'd walked in. He may have been behind Lanaya, but he was clearly the leader.

When he sat, nothing about him moved, except for those black eyes.

Mulder had no doubt that in another time, in another culture, Dugan Velador would have been royal.

Right now, a quivering left hand covered the rattlesnake necklace, while the right hand rested on fingertips on the table. He said nothing, and Mulder kept silent. What amazed him, and puzzled him, was that Lanaya hadn't protested either. He, too, sat with one hand against his chest, the other out of sight in his lap.

It was Scully's concern that broke the silence. She leaned toward Velador, a hand out but not touching. "Mr. Velador, are you all right? I'm a doctor, sir, if you need help."

Mulder could almost hear the neck bones creaking as the old man turned his head. "I'm fine, young woman. It seems that we are not as alone as we thought."

An angry look at Lanaya forced Mulder to gesture, to regain the man's attention. "It wasn't Nick who told me, sir. He didn't . . . he didn't betray a confidence."

"What do you know?"

There was no hesitation; this wasn't the time.

"As much as I'm able without having been in the kiva with you."

"Then you know that what you say can't be true."

Mulder avoided Scully's eyes. "No, sir, I'm afraid I don't know that at all." Although he suspected the old man knew more than he gave away, Mulder told him about the four deaths, described the bodies, and used the same hand motion Nando Quintodo had. "It's the only explanation, sir. Nothing else makes any sense."

That surprised Velador. "You think it makes sense?"

Mulder shrugged—*sure, why not?*

"And you?" he asked Scully gently. "Do you think this makes sense?"

"I think I haven't heard anything else yet that . . . that covers the situation as well."

He smiled then, a broad smile that nearly broke into a laugh. "You look at things differently than your friend."

"Oh yes," she said. "Oh, yes."

Another look to Lanaya, a curious one, made Mulder frown. What had Lanaya done or said that the old man should be so annoyed?

Suddenly Lanaya bent over in a coughing fit, covering his mouth with a loose fist. "Sorry," he gasped, tears filling his eyes. "Sorry. I—" He waggled his fingers at his throat and coughed again, much harder, more harshly. Finally, when he couldn't stop it, he got up and, behind an apologetic gesture to carry on, left the hall, muttering about finding some water. Mulder could hear the awful hacking until the door swung shut behind him.

"He always gets that way when I embarrass him." Velador smiled mischievously. "One day I will have to beat it out of him. He's too old for that sort of thing."

Mulder straightened.

"Mr. Velador," Scully said, "we were told no one would speak to us. Why did you change your mind? Because of—"

"Sometimes I am not as smart as I think I am, you know. Sometimes, sitting in the sun, there is a buzzing in my head, and I don't hear the words everyone says to me very well. Sometimes the words I say are not the words others hear."

"What did you say?"

"I said the FBI must be stopped."

She tapped a knuckle lightly, thoughtfully, against her lips. "Are you saying that now we're in some kind of danger. Just because of that?"

He nodded, then shook his head. "If what this man says is true, young woman, you're in more danger than you know. But not because of what I said."

"Yes," Mulder said suddenly, getting to his feet. "I'm sorry, sir, but you're wrong." He started around the table. "Scully, we have to leave." He beckoned to her urgently, took her elbow when she stood, and nearly dragged her toward the door. "Mr. Velador, please stay inside. Scully and I aren't the only ones who have to be careful."

The old man didn't move.

The necklace rattled; he hadn't touched it.

Once they were outside, Scully pulled her arm free. "Mulder, what's going on? You're acting like a madman."

"You got it, Scully. You hit it right on the nail."

"Then what's—"

"Look."

He swept his hand through the air. Showing her the empty streets. The shuttered windows. Closed doors. No dogs, no chickens, no horses in the corral.

The pueblo was deserted.

Nothing moved but a single sheet, flapping in the wind.

TWENTY-TWO

X Lanaya's pickup was gone.

A curl of brown dust moved down the street, folding in upon itself when the wind began to pick up.

Over the flat roofs, Mulder could see another dust cloud rising and falling like the hump of a lumbering beast, until the wind shoved it against a wall and scattered it.

Scully took a step down, shading her eyes against the sun and blowing grit. A shake of her head when she couldn't find what she was looking for. When she turned toward the Mesa, the wind snapped her hair around her cheeks, momentarily blinding her until she turned again.

"How did they know?" she asked. "It's so fast. How did they know?"

"Someone told them," he answered grimly, and stepped all the way down to the ground. The few vehicles he could see were undoubtedly locked, and he didn't think pounding on doors or windows would get them any help. "We'll have to go back in."

Scully was way ahead of him. She grabbed the large doorknob and tried to turn it over.

It didn't budge.

"Mulder, he's locked us out."

They both tried, and tried using their fists and voices to get the old man to let them in. They stopped when she cursed and massaged her right wrist.

He returned to the street. "Okay, maybe we can find someplace else. A stable or something."

The first place they tried was the warehouse next door, and neither was surprised to find it locked as well. If Ciola is still in there, Mulder thought, he's probably having the time of his life.

They darted across the street and made their way between the two nearest houses to the next street over, saw nothing promising and moved on to the next. By the fourth, he knew they weren't going to find shelter. Not here. And not, he thought as he stared at the Mesa, up there. He didn't know how the Konochine got to the top, but he didn't think they'd take kindly to his trying.

Scully slumped against a house wall out of the direct push of the wind, using a forearm to mop the sweat from her forehead. "Why don't we just wait it out here, whatever it is?"

"We can't, Scully." He stepped away from the house's protection and looked up and down the street. Still nothing. Shutters and doors closed against them. He stretched out a hand and beckoned. "We have to get inside someplace."

"Mulder, it's only a dust storm. We'll need a week of showers when it's over, but it's only a dust storm."

"No. No, it isn't."

And he knew she didn't really believe in the dust storm idea, either. If it were one, they'd be offered shelter somewhere in here; if it were one, the people wouldn't have gone to ground so swiftly. Ciola had told them only a fool stayed outside when the ceremonial was in progress. But since there was no one, not now, they were obviously convinced the Sangre Viento was on its way.

He turned in a slow circle, frustrated, growing angry, beating a hand against his leg while he tried to decide what to do next. Hide, was the obvious answer, but where?

Nowhere.

At least, nowhere in the pueblo.

Apparently Scully had reached the same conclusion. She left the wall's protection and started up the street toward the road, purposeful urgency in her stride. He hesitated before following, hoping she wasn't thinking what he feared she was.

When he caught up, she said, "How far do you think it is?"

Damn, he thought.

"Too far to run. There's got to be someplace closer."

"I have no intention of running, Mulder. At least not yet." She pointed to the fields, and the desert beyond. "If it comes from out there, we'll be able to see it, right?" She gave him a tight smile. "When we see it, then we'll run and see what happens."

"What if it comes from somewhere else?"

"Then we won't have to run, will we."

More leaves, dancing.

When they were close enough, they gave the illusion of a funnel; when they separated they were butterflies again.

Until the sand joined them.

Then they become a cloud.

What Mulder desperately wished he knew, what he couldn't deduce from any of the information he had, was how long it took the whirlwind to form. If it took six men to create one only once in a while over the course of a week, surely a single man, no matter how skilled, couldn't create one with just the snap of a finger.

"Oh God," he whispered as they passed the last house and angled westward toward the road.

Not with the snap of a finger, but after sufficient preparation. Which meant—

Scully, staying on his left, unabashedly using him as a windbreak, picked up the pace as she said, "It's Lanaya, isn't it."

"Yes," he said, more convinced now than he had been that morning.

"Why? Ciola's too obvious?"

"No. Ciola didn't know we were coming today. Lanaya did. He's had time, Scully, to get ready. He took that old man literally. He's going to stop us." He held up a hand before she could interrupt. "He's going to try to stop us, okay?"

She ran a few steps, slowed, ran a few more.

The wind died abruptly.

He couldn't help glancing to the right every few feet, grateful when the fields blocked him, a little apprehensive when he could see all the way to the mountainous horizon. He had no idea what the Wind would look like, or if he'd be able to hear it coming.

He caught up with her when she paused to shake dust from her hair, and grinned when a sudden gust blew it back in her face. "It's a no-win, Scully."

"Tell me about it."

They walked on.

Ahead, above the road, curtains of shimmering heat hung in the air. He took off his tie and jammed it in a pocket. What the hell was he thinking of, wearing a suit on a day like today? And why, he thought further, turning around to walk backward a few steps, didn't he just take his gun, walk up to one of those doors, and threaten to blow the lock off if they didn't let him in?

Because, he answered, they'd probably just shoot back.

Swirls of sandy soil snaked across the blacktop when the wind returned. Rustling made him jump until he realized it was only the corn in its field. A tumbleweed rolled between them, tangling in Scully's feet until she kicked at it savagely and it broke apart, and was blown away.

"Tell me something, Mulder—if this man is so well-liked here, and he can cross successfully between this world and the one out there, why did he do it? Why risk it all?"

They had no water.

His throat was dry, his eyes felt gritty. When he breathed, it was like taking in clouds of fire to his lungs.

They weren't walking nearly as rapidly now.

"He kept saying 'they,'" Mulder answered, licking his lips to moisten them, finally giving it up as futile. "When he gave us that big speech about the Konochine and their dislike of the outside world, he kept saying 'they.'"

He had been one of them until he'd left to go to school. When he came back, he had changed. It was inevitable. And for reasons they might never know, or understand, he hadn't been able to change back, or to adapt as he had adapted to the outside. Mulder suspected it was unfocused anger that forced him to attempt to steal what belonged to the six. They were . . . Dugan Velador was the wise man, the leader. What he did, what the others did, was accepted without serious question.

How could he not want that respect, too?

What he hadn't understood was that the power the old men had came from the respect they were given, not the other way around.

Lanaya figured, have the power, have the respect. That would make him fully Konochine again.

Scully slowed a little, and he saw how her hair had begun to mat to her neck and scalp. He took off his jacket and slung it over his shoulder, his shirt nearly transparent where the sweat held it against his skin. When he brushed his fingers over his hair, the hair felt hot. He would give a lot right now to look stupid in a hat.

Then he blinked, wiped his face, and blinked again.

The gap in the Wall was only a hundred yards away.

He looked back at the pueblo, and saw nothing move. Dust blew through it, and all he could think was *ghost town*.

The dust devil grew and spun in place.

It was little more than two feet high, wobbling around its axis as if ready to collapse should the wind blow again.

Butterflies and sand.

No sound at all.

Mulder stumbled, and Scully grabbed his arm to steady him. He smiled at her wanly. "Isn't that what I'm supposed to do?"

"Since when did you ever think I was helpless, Mulder?"

Never, he thought; never.

They walked into the gap, and into its shadow which was no shade at all. Ahead, the road rose and fell as if it were a narrow wave, making him rub his eyes until it steadied. In his shoes his feet burned, and his ankles promised spectacular blisters once he took the shoes off.

Something small and dark scuttled across the road.

It was tempting, very tempting, to take his shirt off. The cloth was a weight his shoulders could barely handle. The jacket on his arm already weighed a ton, and he didn't think he'd be able to carry it much longer.

"How did they do it?" Scully asked as they came out of the gap and stopped. She stared across the desert floor. They could see no interstate, no trucks, no cars, no planes overhead. There was nothing but the sky and the mountains. "How did they cross this place without killing themselves?"

"They had water, for one thing," Mulder said sourly.

"It must have been incredible," she said. She laughed. "It must have been a bitch."

He let his knees fold him into a crouch, his jacket slipping to the road. There was too much space here, too much sky; gauging distance accurately was nearly impossible, but he seemed to remember that the ranch house wasn't much more than a mile to his right. If they climbed the fence and angled overland instead of sticking to the road, they might make it faster.

He didn't realize he'd been speaking aloud until Scully said, "What if you twist an ankle?"

"Me? Why me?"

She grinned. "I'm a doctor, I know better."

It was heartening to see the smile; it wasn't good to see how her face had reddened. They were dangerously close to sunstroke; they had to be. And dehydration wasn't all that far behind. If they were going to do it, they'd better do it now.

He rose with a groan, and with a groan leaned over to pick up his jacket.

"Ciola is evil, you know," she said.

He draped the jacket over the barbed wire and held it down while she climbed awkwardly over.

"Lanaya is worse."

He didn't get it. "Why?"

"I can understand Ciola. But it'll take me a long time to understand Nick."

As tall as a man.

And now it began to whisper.

He stumbled over nothing, and commanded his limbs to knock it off. It wasn't as if they were in the middle of the desert, a hundred miles from the nearest civilization. He could already see the fences, could already make out the dim outline of the ranch house. A mile, maybe, he couldn't be sure. But he was acting as though it was ten miles, or more.

Scully sidestepped a prickly pear and nearly walked straight into another. She swiped at it with her suit coat, the move turning her in a circle.

"Do you think Sparrow is in on it?"

"What? Sparrow? No, why?"

"He didn't follow us into the reservation, and he wasn't waiting when we came out."

It was too hot to think straight, but he doubted that Sparrow was anything more than understandably skeptical about the whole thing. He was, no doubt, sitting in his office, drinking from his flask, and trying to figure out how he would charm them, or bully them, into getting some credit for the crime's solution. Even if it meant having to accept some magic.

It began to hiss.

It began to move.

"There!" Scully announced. "There it is."

They stood on the lip of a shallow arroyo, beside a hand-crafted bridge.

"Thank God, you see it too," Mulder said. "I thought it was a mirage."

They crossed the bridge single file. The vivid green of the lawn was visible now, and through the rising ghostly heat he could make out the house, if not its details.

On the other side, Scully leaned over the rail. "I think those holes in the bank down there are rattlesnake dens."

Mulder wasn't listening.

He had stopped to take a breath, a brief rest on

his feet. Without much hope, he checked the gap just in case Ciola, or someone, had taken pity on them, and had followed them in a truck. He also checked the top of the hill, just in case the old man was there.

Then he said, "Scully, how fast can you run?"

TWENTY-THREE

 It rose out of the arroyo a hundred yards away.

Mulder had expected it to be shaped like a miniature tornado, but it was conical from top to bottom, and cloudy with the debris that whipped around its surface, the source of the hissing it made as it left the dead river and made its way toward them.

Eight feet high; at least four wide in the middle.

Whether it was the force behind it, or the weight of the sand and grit that formed it, it wobbled as it moved, with thin dark bands rippling along its surface, snapping apart and re-forming.

Every so often a gap would appear and he could see right through it; then the gap would close, swallowed whole.

Had it arrived an hour or two earlier, he didn't doubt they would have had a chance to make it to the house. Its ground speed was not much greater than that of a leisurely trot. Not now, though; not after so much time in the sun.

They ran over the uneven ground as if palsied, as if drunk, veering wildly away from each other, then having to veer again in order not to collide when they tried to rejoin. Serrated grasses slashed at their ankles; shrub and brush stabbed at their arms and legs.

The sun hadn't gone; it was still there, pressing down.

Something exploded in the dirt to Mulder's left, leaving a geyser of dust to hang in the air.

Scully cried out wordlessly in alarm when the top of a cactus shattered as she passed it.

When a third puff rose from the ground a dozen yards away, he realized it was the heavier material caught in the force of it—pebbles, perhaps large twigs; their own weight would eventually fling them out like grapeshot.

They skidded and slid down a short depression.

Mulder glanced back over his shoulder and saw the whirlwind sweep past a small bush, shredding the branches it touched.

Scully grunted and went to one knee, her left

hand crossed over to grip her right shoulder. She'd been hit. Mulder raced over and hauled her to her feet, pushed her on when he was struck behind his right knee. He dropped as she had, then launched himself forward as if from a starting block. His right hand went around her shoulders when he reached her, and they supported each other into another depression, and up again.

The ranch house bobbed not that far ahead.

He could see the white split-rail fence, the grass, and no one on the porch.

They didn't know; they couldn't hear.

"How does it know?" Scully demanded.

It hissed along the ground, moving faster, growing taller.

Growing darker.

Mulder couldn't tell her. He was distracted by the sudden, guttural roar of an engine, searching wildly until he spotted a battered pickup lurch out of a boiling dust cloud to their right.

He was so startled he didn't see the rock until it was too late. His right foot slid over its smooth, flat surface, and he would have gone down had not Scully gripped him tightly and yanked him, still running, back to his feet.

The porch was still empty; what the hell were they doing in there?

Sweat ran into his eyes, blinding him, stinging.

Scully yelled, and he thought for a moment she'd been hit again, and his shoulders automatically hunched in anticipation. When she yelled a second time, he understood; she was trying to get the attention of the house.

It wouldn't do any good.

The hissing was too loud.

Something large snapped not far behind them, like the crack of a huge bullwhip.

The pickup drew closer, jouncing recklessly over the ground, slipping sideways left and right as the driver tried to keep it in line.

Scully finally noticed and waved at it frantically once, but when Mulder tried to steer them toward it, she suddenly shouldered him away. "Him," was all she was able to say.

Nick Lanaya was behind the wheel, and it didn't take long for Mulder to realize that the man wanted to herd them away from the house, to keep them in the open. It was also the answer to Scully's question: since the man hadn't known exactly where they would be, he would have had to keep them in sight once he'd set the Wind in motion.

Someone stepped out onto the porch.

"Almost there," he gasped. "Hang on, we're almost there."

The pickup aimed right for them.

Mulder stubbornly refused to give ground, forcing his concentration on the maddeningly slow approach of the fence and the lawn. It was Scully who threw them aside when the truck roared by, smothering them in a dust cloud that made it impossible for them to breathe.

The Blood Wind swerved.

The hiss deepened to a growling.

He couldn't see anything, but Mulder heard the Wind and urged Scully back to her feet, shoved her ahead of him and pulled out his gun. Not for the Wind, but for the truck, which had swung into a turn so Lanaya could come at them again.

Stalling them.

Dividing their attention between one death and another.

Twenty yards to the fence when Mulder swung his arm around and fired blindly, not expecting to hit anything, just hoping Lanaya would think twice before trying to close again.

The truck didn't stop.

The Wind didn't stop.

Suddenly the ground hardened, and Mulder looked down and realized they had reached the drive.

Scully had already climbed halfway over the fence.

On the porch Nando's wife screamed, and kept on screaming, her hands clutched against her chest.

The pickup charged, and Mulder fired a second time, hitting the windshield on the passenger side, causing Lanaya to swerve, and swerve again to avoid hitting the fence in front.

But the Wind didn't stop.

It hissed across the driveway, forcing him into a move he knew immediately was foolish but was too late to stop—he bolted to his left, away from the house and lawn. But the sight of it so close and the sound of its voice had panicked him, and by the time he was able to think again, Lanaya had turned the truck around.

Scully yelled at him on her knees from the porch, where Nando was now, a rifle in his hands.

The Wind had paused; a stone, a piece of wood, smashed through one of the ranch house windows.

Mulder felt dizzy. The exertion, the heat and the dust, the sound of that thing spinning slowly in place . . . he took a step back and almost fell, staggered sideways and saw Lanaya in the cab, grinning.

Sangre Viento; it moved.

Nando fired at the truck, and a headlight exploded.

It won't make any difference, Mulder thought,

sidling to his left; kill Lanaya, and the Wind will still be there. It has its target now.

He froze.

No; no, it won't.

The Wind brushed against the corner fence post, and sawdust filled the air, some of it showering into the yard, the rest sucked into the spinning.

Lanaya gunned the engine.

Mulder had no choice left but to run straight toward him. If the Wind picked up speed, he would use the truck to stop it; if it didn't, he would stop it anyway.

If he was right.

The Wind moved, and Scully shouted a warning, her own gun out and aiming.

A Wind-whipped stone glanced off Mulder's knee, and he dropped before he knew he'd lost control. He felt the blood before he felt the pain, and the pain stood him up again.

At that moment, both Scully and Nando fired; at that moment, Mulder aimed and fired.

At that moment, Sangre Viento moved, and moved fast.

If I'm right, Mulder thought as he raced as best he could to the truck.

The windshield was pocked with holes and weblike cracks, the engine still ran, and as he grabbed for the door, he saw Nick behind the wheel, his head back, his face covered with running blood.

He saw the whirlwind speeding toward him.

If I'm right, he thought, and yanked the door open, scrambled onto the seat, and reached for Lanaya's throat.

It wasn't hissing now, it was roaring.

He grabbed the rawhide thong around the man's neck and pulled, pulled again as the truck began to rock violently.

Pieces of the windshield began to fall in.

Giving up on the thong, Mulder nearly crawled into the dead man's lap and ripped his shirt open, grabbed the medicine bag and tried to rip it apart. He couldn't, and something slammed into his side, into his shoulder, throwing him against Lanaya's chest and rocking him back.

Metal shrieked.

Glass cracked and shattered.

He held the bag up, as far away as he could, and put a bullet through it, blowing it apart as he threw himself into the well and waited for one of them to die.

TWENTY-FOUR

X "They were all acting," Mulder said.

He and Scully sat at the porch table with Annie Hatch, he with a slick glass of iced tea, Scully with a glass of fresh-squeezed lemonade. They had invited themselves out on their last day, because Mulder felt the woman should know.

"Sparrow wanted us to believe he was either dumb as a post or a hick who was only around for comic relief. Ciola was the macho, I-dare-you-to-touch-me man, but he was terrified because he knew what Nick could do." He took a long drink and sighed. "And Nick didn't think we'd believe for a second in the Sangre Viento. We're trained agents, we deal with solid evidence and behavioral science and the magic we can do ourselves in the lab."

"It wasn't magic, Mulder," Scully said.

He smiled at the lawn. "Suit yourself."

Too many parts of him still stung where he had been struck by missiles hurled by the Wind, and his face was still an alarming red from his sunburn. He had also been right about the blisters.

Scully, too, was walking wounded, but over the past two days, neither of them had had much time to think about it while they filled out reports, filled out more reports, and listened as Sheriff Sparrow figured for the papers and local television news that the pickup had slammed into the fence while trying to run Scully and Mulder down.

The Sangre Viento had died when the contents of Nick's bag were scattered by the bullet.

None of the news people heard that story at all.

Annie poured herself another glass. "You know, I don't think any of my movies ever had so much excitement. I'm rather sorry I missed it."

Mulder looked at her until she had the grace to blush.

"All right, all right, I was scared out of my mind and hiding in the kitchen. And I'm not sorry at all, are you happy?"

He toasted her with his glass, emptied it and pushed away from the table. They had a late-afternoon flight back to Washington, and driving wasn't going to be all that easy.

Scully finished as well, and as she picked up her bag and stood, he saw genuine reluctance to leave the ranch and Annie.

"Fox?" Annie said.

He didn't correct her.

"What happened to Red?"

"We don't know for sure," Scully answered for them. "We think he was trying to conduct his own investigation. From what the office tells us, he was hardly ever there once we arrived. Sparrow admitted to keeping him informed on the phone, but even he hasn't heard from Agent Garson since the night before we went to the Mesa."

"I think he went there on his own," Mulder said, slipping his sunglasses from his pocket and sliding them on. "I think he'll be found before long, but he won't be alive."

Another actor, he thought; the easterners he couldn't stand had come out to conduct what should have been his investigation, and he had to pretend to like it all the way.

They said their goodbyes, and Mulder, if he hadn't already had the sunburn, would have blushed with pleasure when Annie kissed his cheek and made him promise to come back for a visit before she was too old to enjoy it.

They started for the car, but as Scully slid in behind the wheel, Mulder asked her to wait and hurried back to the porch. Annie leaned over the rail when he crooked a finger.

"What is it now?"

He pulled down his sunglasses. "There's a guy over there," he said, pointing toward the Wall. "He sits on that hill and fries himself practically every day. Maybe you ought to go over there sometime and have a talk with him."

Annie stared. "A talk?"

"It's a thought," he said.

"I'm not going back, Fox, if that's what you're asking."

"I'm not," he said innocently. "But there was this guy they thought was a saint, and he turned out to be a thief and a killer. The kids liked him, I understand."

She didn't respond.

"Besides," he added as he pushed the glasses back up, "who says a saint has to be a man?"

She was still on the porch as they drove toward the main road, and he suspected she would be there for some time to come.

He didn't speak until Scully pulled out onto the interstate. "Amazing, wasn't it? The Sangre Viento, I mean."

She glanced over at him, unsmiling. "I'm working on it, Mulder, I'm working on it."

"Of course you are."

Gradually the desert gave way to the first houses, which multiplied and grew taller, and the interstate grew more crowded. Scully had a silent, close to obscene altercation with a pickup that cut them off, and another with an old tail-fin Cadillac that hadn't yet discovered the speed limit was all the way up to fifty-five.

A mile later, she glanced at him and said, "Do you really think it was power he was after? Because he wasn't really part of that world?"

He didn't answer right away.

"Mulder?"

"Yes," he said at last. "Mostly. Power equals respect is an old lure for those who think they don't have either. Ciola is in the warehouse because he knew what Nick would do. And—"

"That's not respect, Mulder, it's fear."

"Sometimes people like that don't, or can't, make a distinction."

A van passed them, music blaring from its open windows.

"Acceptance," Mulder said then.

"What?"

"Acceptance. Power equals respect equals acceptance."

"Equals fear," she added quietly.

He agreed. He also agreed that murder was seldom as uncomplicated as most would believe. He and Scully could probably talk about it all the way back to Washington, and they still wouldn't have the complete answer.

The only one who did was Nick Lanaya.

"Scully," he said while she tried to follow the signs to the airport, "what do you think would happen if, for example, the man who replaces Velador in that circle gets a notion? Like Lanaya did. Lanaya didn't know exactly what went on in the kiva. He made a few guesses, got a few answers from the old man, who didn't know he was giving them, and did the rest on his own.

"What if one of the circle decided to turn mean?"

She didn't answer.

He had no answer.

What he knew was that Nick could possibly have gone on indefinitely, killing those he didn't like, killing those he took a dislike to for no reason at all. He could have, mostly because no one else believed.

He watched the city, the cars, saw an airplane drifting low toward a landing.

Those old men may be wise, but they aren't all old, and none of them is perfect.

Imagine, he thought.

Imagine the power.

The Truth is in here, too . . .

*Turn the page for
special bonus material
related to* **The X-Files!**

Just before the season finale of The X-Files *in 2002,* Gillian Anderson *granted an interview about the end of the series, relaying her thoughts, feelings and inspiration behind the nine hugely successful years of* The X-Files.

(Courtesy of 20th Century Fox Television Distribution)

Everything changed. I was out of work; I was on unemployment; I was living in an apartment, actually, when it was picked up I was living in somebody else's apartment. I had no possessions, I had no car, I mean it changed absolutely everything. I mean, from shooting it out of the country, you know all of a sudden having a home in another country and having a paycheck—let alone a consistent paycheck.

The concept of shooting out of sequence—the scenes out of sequence, not chronologically—all of a sudden was like, "Wait a second. How do you do that?" And I devised a way to write up charts. And I would do this chart of every scene and what information I knew before that, what I didn't know yet, you know, so that I could refer to it.

If I watch the early episodes I see, you know, over time somebody who's starting to put the pieces together and figure out, "Oh, okay. It's better if I turn towards the light in this scene." You know, your body starts to be able to stand back and see what the audience is seeing and then monitor the performance based on that perspective, not about everything being about what I'm doing. So it's interesting what you learn, and all of that was learning in the doing.

I really feel, in a certain way, that I did grow up on camera. It's funny, because child actors have that experience of growing up on camera. Because I started in my 20s, at first I might not just jump to that conclusion. But when I really think about that it was just under a third of my life, and I was still growing, and I was still a baby.

I don't think I had a clear, conscious thought about the chemistry until it started to be brought to my attention by doing press and by people asking, "What about the chemistry between you and David?" It was definitely there; it still is. I mean, there's something that can't be explained about it—there's no rhyme or reason, [laughing] you know, it's just there when we are together in front of the camera.

I love Robert and Anabeth, and they brought some really wonderful work and interesting characters to the show, and I think it was necessary at the time for the show to make that transition into something new and fresh.

I think in terms of high points, I think that writing and directing an episode was one of the greatest high points, and in having subconsciously learned enough in the process of doing and doing and doing that I could then step outside enough to be able to kind of do it myself—certainly with a great deal of help—but to be able to do it myself and be in control, you know, which is really what directing is all about. It's about being in control of all the details.

On July 1, 2008, for the first time ever
in one volume, Harper will publish
THE X-FILES BOOK OF THE UNEXPLAINED,
the ultimate guide to everything you need to know
about "The X-Files" television series, including
pictures, fascinating facts and the true stories behind
the supernatural phenomena on *The X-Files*.

Turn the page for a sneak peek!

AREA 51

"What do you think they are?"
MULDER

*"Everybody thinks they're flying saucers. I think it's some
new Star Wars cybertech hardware. Who knows? They'll
probably roll it out for, like, Desert Storm II . . . "*
EMIL

Observers have reported seeing odd lights, describing maneuvers which appear to be well beyond the capabilities of conventional aircraft—exceptional speeds, abrupt mid-air halts and hovering. Some report sightings of triangular craft and discs.

Aviation Week and Space Technology magazine reported on Area 51 in their October 1, 1990, issue, speculating on "a quantum leap in aviation" and saying: "There is substantial evidence that another family of craft exists that relies solely on exotic propulsion and aerodynamic schemes not fully understood at this time." However, editor and author of the piece, John D. Morocco, later scoffed at the suggestion that the craft were anything but terrestrial in origin on public radio. As Area 51's past record had proven, if anything was possible, it was possible there.

In a 1988 article in *Gung-Ho,* (an American military publication) aviation writer James Goodall had quoted a retired Air Force colonel as saying, "We have things that are so far beyond the comprehension of the average aviation authority as to be really alien to our way of thinking." So was that the only kind of "alien" out at Area 51? It is not hard to rationalize that a "UFO" seen there, more than any other place on the planet, could well be a state-of-the-art experimental craft.

But still the rumors persist—and not just of strange sightings. According to one-time local news anchorman George Knapp, who is also involved in UFOlogy, "stories of captured or acquired alien technology have circulated in the area since the mid-1950s and the beginning of the base." Most were nothing more than rumors—although an insider's claim, in 1953, of a disc-shaped craft whose cockpit was so small that it had to be altered to fit a man, and a daylight sighting of a disc escorted by helicopters in 1978, kept the story alive.

Ten years later, it was stronger than ever. *Gung-Ho* editor Jim Shults acknowledged these stories in 1988, writing: "Yes, I know I sound crazy, but the rumor is awfully solid! Something remarkable has caused the Russians to suddenly want to play ball, and I personally believe this could be it . . . "

No smoke without fire? Unfortunately, before anyone could investigate the fire, it became entirely obscured by the smoke. What had, for most of the decade, been a relatively thin plume of speculation became, at its close, a billowing cloud.

In 1989, Robert Lazar, a technical engineer, appeared on KLAS TV news and made UFOlogical history. He had, he said, worked at Area 51, sector S-4, in a position that was 38 levels above the top secret "Q" clearance that he had held at a previous job working on the Strategic Defense Initiative at Los Alamos National Laboratory. His claims were astonishing. He had been involved in "reverse engineering" the vehicle propulsion system of an extraterrestrial craft.

He described the craft he had worked on as disc-shaped, approximately 30-35 feet in diameter and 15 feet high with a dull aluminium finish. Inside, he said, "It looks like it's made out of wax and heated for a time and then cooled off. Everything has a soft, round edge to it—there's no abrupt changes in anything. It looks like it was cast out of one piece." Lazar said that he was not told how or when the craft—referred to affectionately on base as "The sport model"—had arrived at S-4, but guessed by its appearance that it had not crashed. It was, he said, in working order, and had been test-flown. He added that knowledge of the project was subject to compartmentalized "need-to-know" clearance, and that members of Congress, possibly even the president, would not know about it. (Unless they happened to be watching the news, one supposes.)

For a guy making some outrageous claims, Lazar sounded remarkably credible. It was because he appeared, to the layman at least, to truly know his stuff in the science department. In interviews he convincingly described the concept of non-linear travel, facilitated by a gravity field which distorts space and time, and exactly how the craft's reactor generated such a field.

On the technical side, most of Lazar's claims were not *a priori* impossible—just unprovable. And proof that Lazar did work at Area 51 has yet to be satisfactorily refuted. However, his own credibility was severely thrown into doubt when some of his academic credentials failed to check out, and aspersions were cast on his character when he was subsequently arrested on pandering charges for his involvement in a Nevada brothel.

However, many people believe there is a truth in his claims. British UFOlogist Timothy Good says, "Bob Lazar's story is fascinating and I feel it's essentially true. I think he's lied about his credentials—there's absolutely no evidence that he has any qualifications as a nuclear physicist, but he's a very talented engineer, that's for sure." Indeed, Lazar had built a jet car for fun, and had a particle accelerator in his bedroom—he was that kind of guy. Good muses: "I think he needed to bolster his image to make the story more credible, but of course, once people realize that he's exaggerated about something, they tend to throw the baby out with the bathwater, which, in this case, I don't think we should."

Those who believe that the Government is executing an insidious program to manipulate the public suggest that Lazar may be an unwitting pawn in this plan.

Lazar himself claims that his prospective employers knew a great deal about his background—including his contacts within the UFO community—when they approached him. Not impossible, then, that they even knew about his fudged c.v. The cover-up theorists conjecture that if someone wanted to disseminate information in a way that would reinforce an idea, Lazar would be just the fellow you'd pick for the job—credible enough to command belief and fallible enough to invite doubt.

The problem with government conspiracy theories is that there is one for every occasion: Denials? Lack of evidence? It's a cover-up. A breach of official confidentiality? Indoctrination? Claims which invite ridicule? Deliberate disinformation.

In some cases, of course, the deductions may be right on the button. But, in essence, conspiracy theorizing is just another example of mankind's need to know, to have an explanation for everything. As Jerome Clark, veteran anomalist and deputy president of the J. Allen Hyneck Center for UFO Studies once wrote: "The three hardest words for a human being to utter are *I don't know*."